ET Here Now!

BELIEVE IT OR UFO IT!

By Tucker G. and Grand Bob

Book Cover Artwork and additional book graphics designed by Teddy Whittenbarger, Red Bank, TN.

Published by Spalding Publishing
http://spaldingpublishing.com/

First Edition: 2023

ISBN: 978-1-935803-01-0

Printed in the United States of America

DISCLAIMER

Prepare to delve into an untold narrative that has largely been kept from the American public. As this book unfolds the captivating history of UFOs, your perspective will determine whether you regard it as a work of fiction or nonfiction. Consider this volume a comprehensive introduction to the expansive universe of UFOs and extraterrestrials. It is but a steppingstone on your journey, leading you towards the vast wealth of information awaiting in the wider world.

DEDICATION

This book is dedicated to those sentinel men like AFOSI Agent Richard Doty, Bob Lazar, a nuclear particle US government scientist, Sgt. Clifford Stone, US Army and Airman Charles Hall USAF who came forward to tell the American public of their actual experiences with ET life and UFO technology. (GAIA.com Cosmic Disclosure is a must TV subscription service for UFO info).

We might never had known without these men's personal sacrifices in the face of government or skeptic ridicule and potential physical harm. I also give TV reporter, George Knapp, Sirius Disclosure.com president Dr. Greer and Linda Moulton Howe with her websites Earthfiles.com tremendous credit for their highly organized research into the ET/UFO phenomenon they all have shared to educate the public regarding ETs, UFOs and US reversed antigravity vehicles (ARVs) and zero-point energy for our children's future that the US Government has kept hidden for nearly 80 years.

Greer, Steven M. "10-page summary of witness testimony on UFO facts." WantToKnow.info. Accessed June 2, 2023.
https://www.wanttoknow.info/ufocover-up10pg.

ACKNOWLEDGEMENTS

Jack Gray: "A tremendous book that Proves UFOs and ETs Are Here Now!"

Pendal Myers: "ET Here Now explains a lot of questions I had for years with real answers to the UFO phenomenon."

James T., former Instructor Navigator from Bishop, CA: "If you don't think UFOs are real, get ready for a book full of compelling evidence of their existence."

John Egan: "The topic is intriguing to begin with, the book provides an amazing investigative angle to understand the phenomena."

Brenda M: " *ET Here Now!* goes beyond mere speculation and offers readers a panoramic view of the scientific quest for extraterrestrial life. Author Dr. Spalding delves into the cutting-edge discoveries and ongoing research that fuel our curiosity about other civilizations in the cosmos. Whether you are a skeptic, a believer, or someone in between, *ET Here Now!* will challenge your assumptions and ignite your imagination. It is an invitation to contemplate the vastness of the universe, the possibility of other intelligent beings, and our place within this cosmic tapestry.

ET Here Now! is an enthralling journey that takes readers on a thought-provoking exploration of the vast unknown. With each turn of the page, author Dr. Spading invites us to delve into the captivating realm of extraterrestrial life, sparking our imagination and stretching the boundaries of our understanding."

WARNING: *BEFORE PROCEEDING!*

Nov 11, 2022. The Biden Government FBI just raided a US journalist (Joerg Arnu) in Rachel, Nevada who maintains a website called www.dreamlandresort.com , This website is dedicated to informing the public since 1999 about AREA 51 activities. I highly recommend those who want to get more information about AREA 51, visit this site. However, based on the following article, you need to be warned that the BIDEN administration's FBI may mark you as a US Citizen Troublemaker (CT) and give reason to raid your home and computer just as they did this individual, Joerg Arnu. EVEN purchasing this book, ET Here NOW could put you on a FBI list given the current presidents censorship of our reading material based on BIDENs Ministry of Truth.

Miller, Andrew Mark. "Air Force, FBI Reportedly Raid Homes of Area 51 Website Owner: 'I Have No Choice but to Take Legal Action'." Fox News, November 17, 2022. https://www.foxnews.com/us/air-force-fbi-reportedly-raid-home-area-51-website-owner-completely-unnecessary.

Meads, Tim. "Uh-Oh: Looks Like Biden's DOJ Just Raided An Area 51 Journalist At Gunpoint." Daily Wire, November 11, 2022. https://www.dailywire.com/news/uh-oh-looks-like-bidens-doj-just-raided-an-area-51-journalist-at-gunpoint.

CONTENTS

ET Here NOW!

CHAPTER 1
HISTORICAL ACCOUNT OF UFOS

Prepare to delve into the greatest story never told to the American public. As I recount UFO history, you can be the judge whether this is a book of fiction or nonfiction. This book serves as a primer to the broad universe of UFOs and extraterrestrials and is, but a steppingstone compared to the comprehensive trove of information available in the wider world.

Should you seek proof, I can direct you towards a plethora of media research, interviews, and personal studies, all suggesting that we are not solitary beings in this universe. This book provides more than a hundred links to guide you on this fascinating journey.

Since 1989, I've found myself engrossed in various podcasts, TV shows, and websites, all teeming with UFO narratives. Esteemed individuals like George Knapp and George Noory have been instrumental in my quest for knowledge. I've immersed myself in numerous episodes of Cosmic Disclosure on GAIA.com and followed the intriguing accounts of Richard Doty and Dr. Greer.

I've spent many evenings absorbed in UFO-centric TV shows like UFO Hunters, UFO Witness, and Ancient Aliens. These programs offer illuminating insights into the government's somewhat opaque handling of extraterrestrial matters. I was fortunate enough to engage in a conversation with George Knapp himself, and my bookshelves bear the weight of numerous volumes on the subject.

In my leisure time, you're unlikely to find me absorbed in sports. Instead, my fascination lies with the enigmatic world of UFOs. When I'm not attending to my beloved wife or my grandson, Tucker, I am deeply invested in my research.

My conviction is that the greatest secret of our history is the reality that we're not alone on this planet. I aspire for Tucker to grow up in the knowledge of the existence of real ETs and the potential of UFO technology. I fear our government is more inclined towards creating narratives than revealing the truth, and I do not wish for Tucker to be fed these untruths.

I was born the first week that Eisenhower was elected president of the United States. I didn't know how important that president was until 1989 when I found out that we had been visited by extraterrestrials by the testimonials of the nuclear particle research scientist, Bob Lazar. Believe it or not, according to multiple military and government witnesses, Eisenhower had at least three super-secret meetings with extraterrestrials at California air force bases and signed a major secret treaty with these ETs that involved how they conducted their presence and scientific intentions on earth.

I had many jobs before becoming a podiatrist, specifically working for the government. I worked as a local full-time road deputy and dispatcher on the night shift for 2 years while going to school during the day for a paramedic certification. After receiving my paramedic certification, I left law enforcement for higher pay and worked as a full-time paramedic for a major fire department.

Yet, what truly disconcerts me is the thought of Tucker maturing in a world that's been deprived of its full potential. The young lad deserves to know the truth about the universe we inhabit, the truth about our extraterrestrial neighbors, and the truth about the technological advancements that could shape our future.

In my humble opinion, it's high time humanity acknowledged the reality of advanced beings cohabiting with us. After all, it's not merely about recognizing their existence. It's about embracing the vast possibilities their presence signifies for us all.

Indeed, the extent of evidence supporting the existence of ETs and UFOs is truly remarkable. And the lengths to which the US government has maintained this as a covert matter is equally startling.

So, whether you perceive my narrative as truth or fiction, that decision rests with you. I may tend to emphasize a point, simply to ensure its gravity is not lost. So, sit back, and allow me to guide you through this intriguing journey.

Despite my years spent in conventional medicine, my eyes have been consistently drawn to the skies, ever captivated by the mysterious lights and strange phenomena that I cannot readily explain. Indeed, my grandson Tucker and I have observed peculiarities that don't align with the movements of regular satellites.

We live in a universe teeming with stars, and with the advent of new technologies such as the WEBB telescope, we have identified trillions of them in our galaxy alone. Each star potentially hosts several exoplanets, many of which could potentially foster life. Given the vast age of the universe, it stands to reason that other civilizations may have had billions of years to evolve, visit, and possibly influence our own planet.

Reports from reputable sources such as GAIA.com, Ancient Aliens, and Earthfiles.com suggest that our Earth is teeming with life forms of extraterrestrial origin. We continue to discover new species, hybrid beings, and even off-planet bacteria. Regrettably, this information isn't broadly disseminated to the public.

Recent polls indicate that while a significant number of people accept the possibility of advanced civilizations elsewhere in the universe, they are more skeptical about the notion of extraterrestrials residing here on Earth. However, it's worth noting that those who have researched the topic extensively often hold more nuanced views.

Several renowned astronomers and astrophysicists, who once dismissed the existence of UFOs and extraterrestrials, are now positing that they may indeed be present among us. Some have even been secretly consulted to investigate reported UFO crashes and alleged sightings of aliens on Earth.

The government's persistent efforts to maintain secrecy regarding the UFO and ET presence are deeply concerning. There have been reports of government agents exerting influence over major media outlets to suppress information about UFO sightings, abductions, and other related events.

During a recent interview on Sigourney Weaver, who was the star in the blockbuster movie, ALIEN series told the TV audience a very brave statement on the TV show, Sunday Morning on 9/25/22, "Don't believe what your teachers tell you". She was referring to her teachers at Yale for drama classes that she felt didn't encourage her or felt she should continue acting.

I would personally qualify that statement to mean, "Don't Believe Everything your teachers (or Government) tell you". As some teachers have been sharp and on the mark about UFOs but others have been clueless of don't have anything to share. I am sure we have all had the full spectrum of educators that fits this mold on this subject as well an many other topics.

So, whether you embrace these revelations as truth or dismiss them as fiction, the choice is entirely yours. I may reiterate certain points to ensure they resonate, but ultimately, the interpretation and acceptance of these ideas are in your hands. In the spirit of exploration and the pursuit of truth, let us venture forth into this fascinating realm, hand in hand.

CHAPTER 2
LIFE AMONG THE STARS: AN UNEARTHLY ORIGIN & OUR SHARED HISTORY

In this vast cosmos, our humble Earth is but a tiny speck, and yet, it has been a cradle for an abundant tapestry of life. Among those diverse life forms, we find a connection with beings not of this world - the Extraterrestrials, or ETs, as some might prefer. These celestial inhabitants, I daresay, are far from being strangers to us. Indeed, their presence predates our ancestors' first attempts at cave art. Some of them have found solace in the depths of our oceans, both warm and frigid, while others walk among us on solid ground.

These ETs are extraordinary entities. Over the millennia, they have intricately woven themselves into our DNA, shaping and molding the very essence of our existence. Their scientific prowess far surpasses our understanding; they can cloak themselves and their advanced machinery, assuming the form of the commonplace - a cactus, a human, or perhaps a common creature of the earth.

We should be wary of dismissing ancient tales as mere myths or folklore; these narratives often bear the mark of genuine encounters with these star beings. Even the dinosaurs, those behemoths of a bygone era, may be a testament to the ETs' grand design. They brought with them the genetic codes of these creatures, experimenting, and blending them with our own. This explanation, I assure you, may bear more weight than some of the theories expounded in our esteemed institutions.

Now, let's delve into a bit of clandestine knowledge that the intelligence agencies would prefer to remain concealed. Dr. Greer, a respected figure in this field, posits that it is indeed possible for us to establish direct contact with these Star Beings. This isn't a novel concept, mind you. Various religious groups have been engaging in similar practices since the time of the aboriginals in Australia, dating back some 10,000 years.

Dr. Greer, via his platform, www.siriusdisclosure.com, has devised a meditative method known as CE5. This program closely mirrors the prayer and meditation approaches many religions employ to initiate telepathic communication with these beings.

It's not something you can master overnight, according to numerous meditation instructors. A consistent practice of this specific form of meditation or prayer is crucial. Dr. Greer, I believe, is genuine in his efforts, and provides supporting evidence on his website, asserting that these beings are indeed eager to impart their knowledge upon us. While there have been some who expressed dissatisfaction with their inability to establish contact, many others, both domestically and abroad, have reportedly succeeded.

Individuals like Billy Meier in Switzerland have not only claimed to establish contact but also to enjoy regular visitations from extraterrestrials. Psychics, too, utilize a form of meditation. Law enforcement agencies have had varying degrees of success in deploying psychics to crack murder cases for over a century.

Greer, Steven M. "10-page summary of witness testimony on UFO facts." WantToKnow.info. Accessed June 2, 2023. https://www.wanttoknow.info/ufocover-up10pg.

Wikipedia Contributors. 'Billy Meier.' Wikipedia, The Free Encyclopedia. Last modified date unknown. Accessed June 2, 2023. https://en.wikipedia.org/wiki/Billy_Meier .

Reiser, M., Ludwig, L., Saxe, S., & Wagner, C. (1979). "Evaluation of the Use of Psychics in the Investigation of Major Crimes." Journal of Police Science and Administration 7(1), 18-25. International Assoc of Chiefs of Police. Accessed June 2, 2023. https://www.ojp.gov/ncjrs/virtual-library/abstracts/evaluation-use-psychics-investigation-major-crimes

Peters, Tiffany. "Mysteries That Were Solved by Psychics." Reader's Digest. Accessed June 2, 2023. https://www.rd.com/list/mysteries-solved-by-psychics/

Unfortunately, our governmental system has, in many ways, kept the populace in the dark about these matters. There have even been instances where individuals were explicitly discouraged from attempting to establish contact with alien cultures, as per Dr. Greer's accounts. I am still learning, and while I have not yet succeeded in contacting these entities through meditation, I am cognizant of the fact that this practice requires more dedication and focus than I currently possess. Establishing contact through meditation isn't something everyone can achieve, but there is historical precedence in Asian, Tibetan, and Indian priests having done so for over a thousand years. For further exploration, I'd recommend GAIA.com's Cosmic Disclosure and Dr. Greer's series.

Here's a revelation that's nothing short of extraordinary: we all possess the potential to learn from and consciously communicate with interstellar beings. These beings are part of civilizations, not hundreds, thousands, or millions, but potentially billions of years old. In contrast, humanity, depending on your preferred historical account, is only between 20,000 to 50,000 years old. Our modern iteration is less than 10,000 years old. Our predecessors date back to a million years ago. Compared to other animal species, we're merely a minuscule blip on the evolutionary chart.

It's suggested that the foundations of our species and all religious doctrines originated from these Star Beings, a notion many might struggle to accept. However, numerous religious institutions, including the Catholic Church, have started to embrace this idea, making room for the incorporation of these beings—known by many names like ETs, aliens, visitors, and star children.

Protocols for initiating contact with these beings have existed since the dawn of our civilization. Indigenous populations, including Native Americans, South American tribes, and particularly the long-standing Aboriginal civilizations in Australia, have maintained these protocols. What was once dismissed as tribal myth by our esteemed archaeologists is now recognized as a gross misunderstanding—real, conscious encounters and sightings of shining orbs date back 50,000 years, much before the time of Jesus or the formation of the Bible around 2300 years ago.

The "gods," or ETs, reportedly communicated through conscious channeling, meditation, telepathy, or prayer, as seen in Greek and Roman 'mythologies' and the holy scriptures of religions like Hinduism, Buddhism, Islam, Catholicism, and Christianity. However, some biblical scholars strongly refute the association of UFOs or ETs with the Bible, as presented in Christian resource websites, and even critiqued by the well-respected New

York Times. It's rather amusing when one hears of Richard Doty's OSI team delivering bags of money to media outlets like the NYT to suppress UFO stories or discredit figures promoting UFO theories, such as Erich Von Duniken.

It's also somewhat dubious that Carl Sagan, who reportedly advised government sources on the origin of actual UFO wreckage, critiqued Erich Van Daniken. Given the multitude of Bible versions written by men inspired by God, it seems even this subject is suspect—much of human history is speculative. Ultimately, the Origin of Man boils down to whom you choose to believe and your personal faith.

OpenBible.info. 'What Does the Bible Say About Ufos?' Open Bible, 2023. https://www.openbible.info/topics/ufos.

Griffiths, George. "UFOs in the Bible? Retired pastor says so." Pressconnects. Last modified October 30, 2017. https://www.pressconnects.com/story/news/connections/faith/2017/10/30/ufos-bible-retired-pastor-says-so/803936001/.

Ankerberg, John, and John Weldon. "Are UFOs Mentioned in the Bible? - Part 2." The John Ankerberg Show. June 10, 2022. https://jashow.org/articles/are-ufos-mentioned-in-the-bible-part-2/.

Joseph, Daniel Isaiah. n.d. "Does the Bible Talk about Aliens and UFOs? (Assess the Claims)." Christianity FAQ. https://christianityfaq.com/bible-aliens-ufos/.

Lingeman, Richard R. 1974. "Erich von Daniken's Genesis." The New York Times, March 31, 1974, sec. Archives. https://www.nytimes.com/1974/03/31/archives/erich-von-danikens-genesis.html.

Gaia. 2020. "Are the Gods and Angels of the Bible REALLY Extraterrestrial Beings?" YouTube. https://www.youtube.com/watch?v=U5lVPUDRCN4.

On the topic of the US Military's disinformation politics towards the public and legislative branches, according to Richard Doty, a former AFOSI counterintelligence officer, carefully crafted disinformation campaigns start with 5-10% truth. Millions worldwide have come forward with evidence of ET visitors dating back thousands of years. The Catholic Church and Christianity have concealed this truth in Vatican libraries for centuries. The reality is, we're a nascent civilization compared to our Star Being counterparts who constantly monitor us.

The lives of thousands of families and numerous credible UFO and ET witnesses have been upended over the past seven decades by US military and intelligence agencies in their relentless pursuit to suppress the truth. The infamous Men in Black would employ tactics of denial, discredit, disinformation, and defamation against anyone who dared to challenge them. This disinformation program has been highly effective for decades, but the veil is gradually lifting with each passing day.

The military's tool of choice isn't solely confined to civilians; it extends to seasoned active-duty personnel as well, to stifle discussion within the ranks. In the past, all military officials had to do was label you a "UFO nutcase," or in today's more politically correct terms, a "consumer," and society would take over the job of ostracism for them. Fortunately, technologies derived from ETs, such as the computer chip, night vision, and cell phones, have helped the public document the existence of ETs in recent decades.

Historically, many world religions and monarchies have persecuted those who sought the truth, condemning them to the stake, the cross, financial ruin, and even stripping them of their children to be raised by the very same secret governmental factions that denied the existence of ETs in the first place.

Chilling Evidence of UFOs | Unidentified: Inside America's UFO Investigation (S1, E3) | Full Episode." n.d. Www.youtube.com. Accessed June 2, 2023. https://youtu.be/k7zzwEXHtA4.

Mason, Michael. 2008. "Burned at the Stake for Believing in Science." Discover Magazine. Discover Magazine. August 20, 2008. https://www.discovermagazine.com/the-sciences/burned-at-the-stake-for-believing-in-science.

UFOs and Extraterrestrial Life - the Aetherius Society." 2011. The Aetherius Society. 2011. https://www.aetherius.org/ufos-and-extraterrestrial-life/.

In the grand scheme of things, our planet is but a fledgling civilization, just beginning to awaken to the larger cosmic community that surrounds us. This shift in consciousness may be disconcerting for some, but it is an inevitable evolution in our understanding of our place in the universe. As we peel back the layers of secrecy, disinformation, and ridicule that have shrouded this topic for so long, we become better equipped to embrace our cosmic neighbors and the broader implications of our shared existence.

Time and space, to these ETs, are not impassable barriers but mere steppingstones. They navigate these dimensions with ease, able to glimpse into the past and future, to traverse different dimensions, and perhaps even exist in several simultaneously. The whispers tell of our own government attempting to harness such abilities back in the late '50s.

However, it's important to remember that ETs, despite their advanced abilities, are not infallible. They have had their mishaps here on Earth. These star visitors have been noticed by humans across the globe for countless generations. Oftentimes, they were revered as angels or deities, for people lacked the language to describe them accurately.

These Star Friends, as I affectionately call them, traverse the universe through wormholes or black holes, propelled by curiosity about us, just as we are about them. Much like us, they harbor beliefs in higher powers.

A quiet understanding exists among many that the government has kept the ET and UFO phenomena under wraps, guided by an old Brookings Institute report. This report cautioned that the revelation of intelligent extraterrestrial life could precipitate the collapse of societies, akin to past civilizations overwhelmed by a superior force.

Our shared history with the Star Friends is a fascinating tale, filled with intrigue and wonder. It began in 1941 in Cape Girardeau, Missouri, when a flying saucer crashed, providing the locals with their first brush with the surreal. This mysterious event stirred the pot of UFO lore.

In 1942, the City of Angels found itself in the throes of an inexplicable event - the Battle of Los Angeles. Anti-aircraft guns lit up the sky, targeting an unidentifiable object floating above. Was it a wayward weather balloon, or were our Star Friends simply on an innocent midnight exploration? Supposedly, a craft was brought down according to one military personnel.

Fast forward to 1947, to a little place named Roswell, New Mexico. This is a name that reverberates through the annals of UFO history. When a rancher discovered strange debris scattered across his property, the military hastily dismissed it as remnants of a weather balloon. Yet, about 600 eyewitnesses of a downed alien spacecraft have kept the story alive through the decades.

In the same year, Truman established the National Security Act, birthed the Central Intelligence Agency and created the Majestic 12 with Admiral James Forrestal to protect the newly acquired alien technology. One can't help but ponder whether they had more insight into our celestial neighbors than they were willing to divulge.

By 1952, Washington, D.C. had its own close encounter. Unidentified objects whizzed across the sky at an alarming speed, prompting the scrambling of jets and causing quite a stir among the populace. The government attributed the phenomenon to temperature inversions, but many continue to speculate that it was our Star Friends gracing our capital with their presence.

Every US leader since the era of Roosevelt and Truman has been privy to information on extraterrestrial activity, regardless of whether they choose to acknowledge it publicly. Bill Clinton, for instance, has conveyed a deep sense of frustration in multiple speeches about his lack of knowledge on UFOs, which can be questioned, considering his infamous track record of denying the undeniable.

However, it must be acknowledged that the extent of knowledge on the UFO phenomenon varies among presidents. Jimmy Carter, for example, confessed to having been given limited information while in office, and later rescinded his willingness to divulge details about UFOs due to what he referred to as "military implications."

The Battle of Los Angeles." 2020. Cal@170 by the California State Library. February 1, 2020. https://cal170.library.ca.gov/february-24-1942-the-battle-of-los-angeles-2/.

National Security Act | United States [1947]." 2019. In Encyclopædia Britannica. https://www.britannica.com/topic/National-Security-Act.

Jimmy Carter Files Report on UFO Sighting - HISTORY." n.d. Www.history.com. https://www.history.com/this-day-in-history/carter-files-report-on-ufo-sighting

Presidents, like Ronald Reagan and Richard Nixon, were given extensive briefings on the subject, while the Bush family, known for their tight-lipped approach, were privy to a wealth of knowledge, with George H.W. Bush having served as a former CIA director. John F. Kennedy, feeling left in the dark by the "Military-Industrial Complex" that Eisenhower had warned about, established NASA to bypass this information bottleneck. There are claims suggesting a direct link between Kennedy's assassination and his intent to disclose ET-related information, which was allegedly scheduled to occur ten days before his untimely demise.

There's a lingering fear among presidents that the fate of the Kennedys, allegedly linked to their intent to divulge ET-related secrets, could befall them, discouraging them from sharing this crucial information. Every president since FDR has been briefed about the ET/UFO presence here on earth, and each one has withheld this information from the public, information that includes the existence of ETs, UFOs, and reverse-engineered US antigravity technology.

Acknowledging the presence of extraterrestrial entities with more control over our future than a US president could lead to a loss of faith, allegiance, and confidence among the American public. Yet, this book suggests that the first president who discloses this ET/UFO information would not only restore public trust in the government but also propel humanity to the stars with the help of extraterrestrial reverse-engineered technology. It is crucial to persuade our politicians to release this information.

Many politicians are left in the dark, and no president can fully comprehend all the technology involved, a feature designed to protect Special Access Projects (SAPs). To this day, there are private citizens who have dedicated their lives to researching this topic and possess more knowledge on this subject than virtually any congressman or senator. But this dynamic is slowly changing as legislators are starting to take seriously the knowledge of individuals like Richard Doty and Bob Lazar.

Standard, Business. 2015. "Aliens Planned John F. Kennedy's Assassination, Claims Author." Www.business-Standard.com. March 23, 2015. https://www.business-standard.com/article/news-ani/aliens-planned-john-f-kennedy-s-assassination-claims-author-115032300193_1.html.

Corroborating UFOs

How can we validate the existence of UFOs? Evidence of extraterrestrial activity has been present throughout history, and more so in the past century. The truth of this is conspicuous if one chooses to look and believe in the credibility of the sources over the years. The government's success in maintaining a veil of secrecy around the development of the Atom Bomb during WWII is a testament to their ability to keep secrets.

Spaceships, more commonly referred to as alien craft, flying saucers, and UFOs, have had incidents of crashes and intact landings on our planet for millennia. There was a reported discovery of a 50,000-year-old UFO during a dinosaur excavation in the Badlands. The area was quickly closed off and the UFO was relocated to a nearby Air Force Base.

In England, a highly advanced aluminum landing tripod foot (Wedge of AIUD) was unearthed 30 feet deep and has been dated between 10,000 BC to 50,000 BC, depending on the group conducting the soil analysis. Aluminum was not produced on earth until 1886. These ET crafts have had incidents on every continent, and not only the US, but China and Russia have also recovered these crafts. The most advanced military industrial nations all reportedly have antigravity programs.

The US has arguably achieved more than other nations in mastering antigravity, but the inventors who were already aware of its possibility have been curbed from reaping any benefits. Their patents have been classified under national secrecy act programs, preventing the public or others from gaining from this technology. The moment to unveil this antigravity technology to the existing classified military aerospace network will be timed carefully to avoid public outrage.

Nuclear UFOs Revealed | Unidentified: Inside America's UFO Investigation (S2, E3) | Full Episode." YouTube. https://www.youtube.com/watch?v=p_MXDxH9Fs0.

Cosmic Disclosure." 2019. Gaia. 2019. https://www.gaia.com/series/cosmic-disclosure.

Ancient Aliens: The Wedge of Aiud (Season 12, Episode 2) | History." n.d. Www.youtube.com. https://www.youtube.com/watch?v=U_frFFyqvww

As intelligent beings, we must come to terms with the fact that humans did not evolve independently on Earth. We are all learners in life and need to restart our understanding from the beginning, including reevaluating human history considering the ET presence.

In researching my numerous books, I've delved into a variety of topics. However, this book, which supports the ET phenomenon, is a more challenging endeavor due to the diversity of opinions. According to a July 6, 2021, Axios poll, the majority of Americans believe in the existence of extraterrestrial life, with 51% of the respondents agreeing that the recent military videos of UFOs provide proof of their existence on Earth. Around 76% of adults under 30 believe that intelligent life exists on other planets, compared to 57% of those aged 50 and above.

This book is unlike any other.

Some readers will accept the information in this book, while others will find reasons to reject the facts presented, based on their upbringing, education, or direct experiences.

While I personally have never had an encounter, abduction, or exposure to a live alien that I am consciously aware of, the recent disclosures about alien-human hybrid programs by credible sources make me wonder if some people have had past encounters without realizing their ET hybrid status.

We often forget that all human races on Earth are newcomers in the vast cosmos, a playpen filled with star beings who either brought us here or modified us here on Earth and influenced our evolution. Consider the potential exposure to new physics, new genetic/DNA science, new medical science, and the ability to traverse time and multiple dimensions that these star beings have mastered and have secretly shared with our government.

65% of Americans Believe in Aliens, New Poll Finds." Axios. July 6, 2021. https://www.axios.com/2021/07/06/aliens-exist-poll.

My entire generation has been deprived of this advanced technology. I attempted to rationalize the trade-off between our enemies obtaining this technology and sharing it with our own citizens. I understand all technology eventually disseminates to other countries, and this would be no exception. Several successful Hollywood movies, such as *Men In Black* (MIB), Close Encounters of the Third Kind, ET The Extraterrestrial, and When the Earth Stood Still, have reportedly been influenced by actual military or CIA information found in various UFO/ET books.

Gene Roddenberry, the creator of Star Trek, was allegedly given actual scripts by the CIA, based on our real-world experiences with antigravity technology, our alien reproduction vehicles (ARVs), and live ET visitors. The CIA has used public entertainment to gauge our tolerance for the idea that humans are not the most intelligent beings in the cosmos.

Furthermore, many Air Force Bases, such as Kirtland AFB, Holloman AFB, Wright Patterson AFB, Edwards AFB, Los Alamos, and many bases within The Nevada Test Site, otherwise known as Nellis Air Force Testing Range, including Area 51 and the Tonopah Missile Range, have reportedly had multiple encounters with ET visitors and ET landings.

There are reports that some of the crashed UFOs are highly toxic and that many military retrieval teams have been killed while approaching these crippled alien crafts with deceased aliens. In some instances, we have even buried these crafts using nuclear underground detonations.

The sources of this information come from various professionals who have had direct contact with ETs throughout their lives, knowledge that has been kept secret for far too many generations.

Earth has been a haven for many ET species. Each ET species consists of multiple races, just as we have here on Earth. There have been confessions from individuals within our clandestine intelligence agencies about paying off media outlets to suppress stories on UFOs or ET contact over the years.

Special Investigations Agent: Richard Doty." n.d. Gaia. https://www.gaia.com/video/special-investigations-agent-richard-doty.

Targeted Disinformation." n.d. Gaia. Accessed June 2, 2023. https://www.gaia.com/video/targeted-disinformation.

I want my grandson to have access to this knowledge and the ability to communicate with ETs himself. I wish I could demand a refund for all those years spent in school learning false narratives about human history and religion. The same government that I respect and pay taxes to has led hundreds of millions of Americans, and billions worldwide, down a rabbit hole, depriving them of the rightful knowledge needed to solve global issues.

While I understand the argument for national defense, I find it hard to reconcile that the same government that has allowed millions of illegal aliens into our country is worried about our enemies gaining this technology. At the same time, they justify hiding the secrets of the universe for another hundred years if they could.

The same technology that was gifted to us by ETs like fiber optics, lasers, Kevlar, night vision, integrated circuits, is now being used to document the existence of ETs (See retired major Philip Corso's Book, The Day After Roswell and his video testimony on Dr Greer's websites www.SirusDisclosure.com who was present and in charge during the Roswell incident).

As our government withholds advanced technology from us, it is paradoxically funding the training of our potential adversaries (China) on how to develop nuclear weapons that could potentially be used against us.

For every person who reports an ET encounter to MUFON, the media, or a relative, whether through direct contact or a visual sighting, there are thousands more who keep the experience to themselves or quietly document it using cell phone cameras. Project Blue Book, the U.S. Air Force's systematic study of UFOs, failed to provide an explanation for roughly 800 of over 12,000 reported incidents, indicating that about 1 in 20 sightings remain unexplained.

NBC News. 2022. "Scientists at America's Top Nuclear Lab Were Recruited by China to Design Missiles and Drones, Report Says," September 22, 2022. https://www.nbcnews.com/news/world/scientists-americas-top-nuclear-lab-recruited-china-design-missiles-dr-rcna48834.

"Waste of the Week on the National Desk: US-Funded Military Research Going to China." n.d. Open the Books. Accessed June 6, 2023. https://www.openthebooks.com/waste-of-the-week-on-the-national-desk-us-funded-military-research-going-to-china/.

This book will serve as a beacon for those who are open to the possibility of extraterrestrial life, providing facts, testimonials, and expert opinions. While some will embrace the information presented, others may reject it, influenced by their upbringing, level of education, or personal experiences.

I confess that I have never had a contact experience, an abduction experience, or exposure to a live alien that I was consciously aware of. However, with the growing number of credible individuals stepping forward to disclose information about alien hybrid human programs, I realize that many people may have unknowingly encountered these entities. This realization has led me to question if some individuals may have had past contact but are currently unaware of their ET hybrid status.

As we continue to explore the evidence of UFOs, it is important to remember that we are still in the early stages of understanding the universe and our place within it. There is much to learn and relearn about human history and our relationship with the cosmos. The introduction of the ET presence in Earth history will undoubtedly lead to a complete transformation of our understanding of ourselves and our world. This book is a small step on the path towards enlightenment.

Our intertwining history with these celestial entities isn't confined to hushed conversations and conspiracy theories. Rather, it is a vibrant thread woven into our collective past, contributing to the rich tapestry of our species' narrative. It is a chronicle of unusual incidents and inexplicable phenomena, of encounters with the unknown and our enduring quest to understand our place in the grand scheme of the universe. And it serves as a reminder that we might not be alone in the cosmos as we once believed.

CHAPTER 3
BELIEVE IT, OR UFO IT

Believe it or not, the narrative tapestry of extraterrestrial encounters is richly woven with accounts of beings and creatures capable of astounding feats. Witnesses report entities that can morph their forms, fabricate DNA clones or hybrids, and "shape-shift" into nearly any figure - be it animal, human, humanoid, or even mythical creatures such as werewolves, dragons, and extinct dinosaurs. Such enigmatic sightings may well correlate with reported sea monsters like Loch Ness and Champ, adding further mystery to these cryptic encounters.

This broad spectrum of alien life forms varies greatly depending on the source. Some credible voices speak of up to 87 different species, while others identify five distinct categories. The actual number, however, is likely beyond our current comprehension, given the trillions of stars that exist in the universe. For the sake of discussion, let's conservatively estimate 57 species, grouped into five categories. Yet, considering alien subspecies, hybrids, and the possibility of genetic modifications, the real number has increased to 7 categories.

In Craig Campobasso's most interesting book, The Extraterrestrial Species Almanac the author states that there are over 1 million civilizations in the known universe. The author lists the specific description and location of each category of alien species. This ET book correlates with many other former government intelligence employees and ufologists.

This vast diversity of extraterrestrial life might be influenced by a multitude of factors. The respective alien's evolutionary history, the risk of extinction, the location of their home planet in relation to their star, exposure to DNA-modifying radiation, and even the availability of food and water could all play a role. Other factors could include natural disasters, alien wars, (this has supposedly taken place on this planet multiple times in the past in India, and Egypt and in South America) and countless other parameters.

I wholeheartedly invite you to delve into this subject and form your own perspective. The evidence supporting an extraterrestrial presence on Earth is compelling and, in my view, irrefutable. As someone who has spent a lifetime studying science and medicine, I believe it's evident to anyone who examines historical evidence objectively that extraterrestrial beings have been interacting with Earth for millennia.

The narrative of human history requires a significant overhaul, as the academic theories no longer align with the mounting evidence for alien interaction. The Fu Fu's, through their whimsical narratives and enigmatic characters, attempt to help our youth explore these intriguing mysteries, fostering a new generation of curious minds ready to challenge existing narratives and uncover the truth of our shared cosmic history.

CHAPTER 4
TUCKER AND HIS EXPERIENCES

My grandson Tucker who is nine years old at the time the first draft of the book was written in 9/22. Tucker was 8 y/o when went to Sedona in May of 2021 to participate in UFO watching (from Johnny UFO tours) in the evening and he saw many objects in the sky with 3rd generation military night vision. These possible UFOs had unusual paths across the sky that started typically as most orbiting satellites and then made angular corrections that were not typical, or they speed up and slowed down. He also got to see three potential portals that next day.

Finding AREA 51 entrance is not simple if you don't live in that area. First, the cell reception and phone reception are blocked by the government when you enter within an estimated 10 miles of the nearest entrance. No road signs are visible and only a long non-descript ten-mile extremely dusty road is your ride to glory. Did I say dusty? I MEAN there was so much DUST on the windows you had to use a wiper front and back to see out. If you run out of gas, get a flat or have a 911 emergency, good luck and GOD bless you. You walk until someone sees you or dies of dehydration. We always had a case of water with us. There is an ominous sign at the south gate that buffalos you first with less than inviting consequences (see below with Tucker) if you proceed past that sign, but the real gate is another 1500 feet past it. You can read what happens if you decide to bum rush or tip toe past the gate, see.

"UFO or Satellites (IFO, IAP or UAP) Sedona,AZ 5/28/21 You Decide." n.d. Www.youtube.com. Accessed June 6, 2023.
https://www.youtube.com/watch?v=jUm5nFxr8Rs&t=15s.

Our journey began at the mystical Portal at Sedona, followed by reassuring normal Geiger readings at the enigmatic Area-51, marking the start of our adventurous 10-mile drive into the facility.

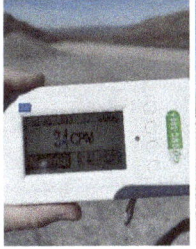

Along the way, we were greeted by the iconic Extraterrestrial Highway sign near Rachel, NV, before reaching the secretive East Gate of Area-51, where we found an intriguing alien skull.

Next, we encountered the South Gate, where Tucker enjoyed a UFO tour in Sedona, AZ. Near one of the mysterious "portals," we registered normal readings on a Tri-field meter, suggesting the absence of unusual signals.

Throughout our exploration, EE&G security guards, in their characteristic white SUVs, vigilantly watched over us from a hill at the South Gate of Area-51.

What Happens if you violate the Perimeter 1000 yards from main south gate, Buffalo sign. The Sign Says:

WARNING

IF YOU ARE CONSIDERING TRESPASSING ON THE NEVADA AND TRAINING RANGE BOUNDARY, PLEASE CONSIDER THE FOLLOWING CONSEQUENCES:

1. YOU WILL BE REQUIRED TO PAY A $1000 DOLLAR FINE.
2. YOU WILL HAVE YOUR CAR TOWED.
3. YOU WILL HAVE YOUR CAR IMPOUNDED AT YOUR EXPENSE.
4. YOU WILL BE BROUGHT TO HIKO, NV TO BE PROCESSED.
5. ONCE RELEASED YOU WILL BE RESPONSIBLE FOR YOUR TRANSPORTATION TO YOUR NEXT DESIRED TRAVEL LOCATION.

As soon as we started to turn around after reading this sign, a travel tour van from Las Vegas sped past us to the next and final south gate area. I immediately got in behind them and drove on another 1500 feet past this sign. The armed ex-military security guards on a hill just 1000 yards NE of this sign were probably laughing and have a running bet to pass the time to see who turns around at the first sign.

Tucker finally got to see the remote Nellis AF Testing range's Area 51 firsthand from the south and east gates. He found an "alien skull" from a visitor at the south gate. He got to see all the Tri-field meter testing and Geiger counter testing I did at the front gates of each location including the Tonopah missile range. To the Government's credit, at every military base gate site, all road stops in Arizona, Nevada, and California's Death Valley, I found no evidence of ionizing radiation higher than the normal background radiation at my home.

The only time the Tri-field meter pegged out big time on the RF selection was at the east gate of A-51 from what I assumed was microwave transmissions which I thought I imagined it felt uncomfortably "hot" like it cooked my right forearm arm. But I can't begin to confirm or suggest that it was a microwave deterrent weapon. I do have a video of that meter reading pegging out though. The Magnetic selection of the Tri-field found a metallic hit likely an underground sensor at the east gate just to the left of the rental car.

We did not go to the north gate as our timeline only allowed us to visit select areas. We went to the Tonopah missile range and the Warms Springs Café (next page) where a live alien capture took place nearby according to AFOSI agent, Rick Doty. An unconfiscated picture of the live alien hung on the wall for over a decade before the café closed.

"Area 51 TriField Meter & Geiger Counter Readings at the East Gate of Area 51." n.d. Www.youtube.com. Accessed June 6, 2023. https://youtu.be/ATq7olPGHG8.

"Special Investigations Agent: Richard Doty." n.d. Gaia. Accessed June 6, 2023. https://www.gaia.com/video/special-investigations-agent-richard-doty?fullplayer=feature.

If ETs or UFOs seems like too advanced topic for his age that might create fear, consider every school child his age has been fearful and sheltered from school for the past two years wondering if their parents, their siblings', grandparents, or their friends might die from COVID. So comparably UFOs and ETs are a much safer topic to learn about.

Certainly, ETs are a much safer topic than indoctrinating kids under 18 about worrying if they were born in the wrong body or the kids in the 50s and 60s worrying daily about nuclear holocaust hiding under their desks in school during an atomic bomb drill. Imagine today's children of Ukraine what they endure daily to learn and how our children react when they show war strife kids on TV news almost daily.

However, with the current Putin-Russian-Chinese threat let's add that worry to our children's backpacks they carry to school every day. At least the ET/UFOs that are here now represent learning about advanced cultures and thinking how to stop all the children's mental carnage we help on them and find new scientific solutions to the human tragedies we repeat. Pollution free travel anywhere, zero-point energy and medical advancements that represent future technology jobs for our kids in the future is what we need to be sharing with our children today.

Tucker certainly doesn't understand all the ET/UFO knowledge or even 2% of it but he has been exposed to more than an average 8–9-year-old. He has drawn some pictures of his knowledge and experiences with ETs and UFOs.

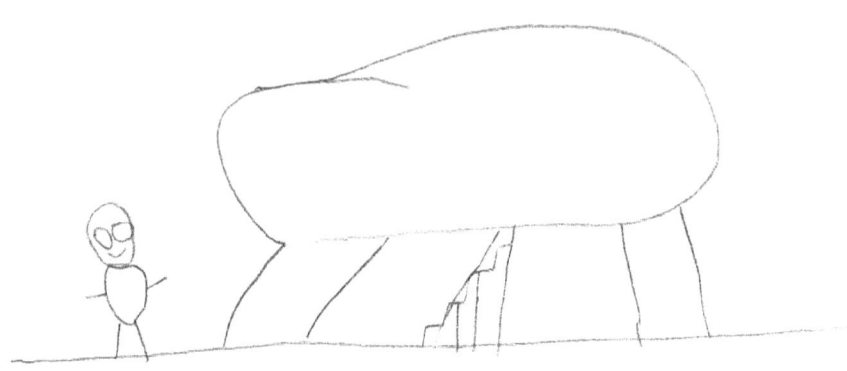

Skinny BOB

According to the US government, they have no knowledge of UFOs at all so I guess Tucker knows more than the US government, so he will get quoted first.

CHAPTER 5
ENCOURAGEMENT FOR OUR YOUTH AND THE HISTORICAL ACCOUNTS OF THE FU FU'S

I would like to offer a message of hope and inspiration to all the young people in America. We live in an era of remarkable technological advancements, with an inexhaustible reservoir of knowledge being cultivated daily for our defense. These advancements, particularly in areas such as antigravity and pristine energy technology, promise a future filled with innovation for hundreds of thousands, if not millions, of years. We are on the precipice of a world where pollution-free energy can be harnessed from the air and space around us for an entire lifetime. I urge you all to strive to uncover these secrets, for they will shape your future.

In light of this, as a means to help the youth navigate these complex scientific realities and possibilities, I was inspired to write a series of books – starting with *The Kingdom of Fu Fu's*. This series isn't merely a collection of stories, but a blend of joy, wisdom, and hidden truths, designed to help young readers grapple with the mysteries of the universe.

The central characters, the Fu Fus, are ancient beings, in existence longer than humans. They have a fascinating story to share, a significant revelation that will surely captivate your interest. The Fu Fus were not the first dwellers of our blue planet. Before them, Star Beings, the cosmic wanderers, sowed the seeds of human life here on Earth.

This secret, among others, is what the Fu Fus are waiting to share with our young generation. Our children, blessed with a wonderful sense of wonder and an open mind towards the miracles of the universe, are the ideal audience for these tales. My hope is that through the accounts of the Fu Fu's, our youth will not only learn about our shared cosmic history but also develop a curiosity and understanding about the existence of Extraterrestrial life and Unidentified Flying Objects.

CHAPTER 6
PHASES OF CONCEALMENT: THE UFO ENIGMA AND THE ART OF INSTITUTIONAL MISDIRECTION BY THE GOVERNMENT

Historical, actual, factual direct phrases, misdirection's and outright lies that the US government, American Presidents or other government officials who still use these deceptive and outright false statements to this day in 2022. I should like to extend to you an amicable warning. You see, as we traverse this complex tapestry of government response and rhetoric, there might be instances where I, in the spirit of scholarly jest and satirical commentary, may provide certain responses that appear to poke fun or perhaps even lampoon the statements of our good government. The nature of our discourse, I'm afraid, can't help but lend itself to such treatment.

Understand, this isn't an act of insolence or disrespect, but rather a reflection of the occasional absurdity of official pronouncements, and an attempt to shine a light on the obfuscations and artful dodges employed by those in power. After all, sometimes humor is the best way to illustrate the gravity of the situation.

The US Government has said for 70 years they don't have any information about UFOs or ETs on Earth so basically the Fu Fu and Tucker knows more than the government by the US Government's own admission. Our government today certainly operates a lot easier if the government can keep the general population operating at a less than intelligent level. The real academic truth of ET life existing on earth has factually been kept under layers of lies and disinformation by our government, just so we don't ask more questions.

For those more intelligent questions that emerge, the most effective government technique is to question if they suffer from a psychiatric history or make inappropriate or satirical references to discredit the public's real UFO sightings or ET abductions.

PHASE ONE

The good news is those days of government disinformation i.e., complete denial or Phase One is quickly coming to an end after 70 years due to civilian's access to sensitive instrumentation and recording devices like HD cell phones, digital cameras, night vision and infrared technology.

PHASE TWO

The US government is now in Phase Two drip feeding the public tidbits of the truth of Tic Tacs and approved well-known navy combat pilot gun camera videos. Phase two will continue for years or until the enlightened members of congress subpoena UFO/ET accountable people like Richard Doty in the congressional witness box. The government is trying to execute a slow walk to the visible end of the pier to halt the inevitable public anger that is building as we get closer to uncovering truth and accountability. Pseudoscience college programs are now being allowed to prepare the public for some banal form of disclosure starting with "alien" bacteria first that has already been confirmed on Mars.

PHASE THREE

This comes with the "polished" ET/UFO disclosure mix of information and disinformation. The intelligence community will assign another false history of the ET/UFO phenomenon with the "new discovery" of antigravity technology. Ultimately however, this disclosure and release of AG technology and zero-point energy (ZPE) will completely change the current structure of government in so many ways.

"'We Cannot Afford to Be Ill Prepared': Research Hub Wants to Prepare Humanity for Potential Proof of Alien Life." 2022. CTVNews. November 7, 2022. https://www.ctvnews.ca/sci-tech/researchers-in-scotland-want-to-prepare-humanity-for-potential-proof-of-e-t-life-1.6142956.

Remember, The Government has trillions of reasons to lie about ETs and UFOs. Disclosure on this subject is going to first expose many trillions of taxpayer dollars that have been diverted to black projects, USAP's and payoffs to the entire Media industry. Hollywood will have a field day with that conspiracy film angle. That is also a bit hypocritical as Hollywood has benefited by our intelligence whistleblowers releasing truth in fact ET/UFO scripts that have also made the movie industry wealthy. Perhaps this exposure of disclosure will result in real benefits that other governmental agencies have kept for themselves.

Other Governments around the world are a lot more forthright to their public about the UFO phenomenon such as: France, Belgium, Peru, Chile, Argentina, and many other nations who share this information. China has a very active UFO group that has one million active members and growing. I still use the term UFO and not UAP or Unidentified Aerial Phenomenon because the original UFO term is more historically accurate, more well known, much more appropriate and is where all our research exists when conducting older freedom of information searches.

The UFO term was started by Donald Keyhoe a US marine aviator, author, and a major UFO supporter who wrote some of the first UFO books, Flying Saucers Are Real (1950) and Flying Saucers from Outer Space (1953). Keyhoe had one of the first national TV broadcast on UFOs on the Armstrong Choice Theatre where the audio feed was blocked by sudden static when he discussed the fact, he believed flying saucers were real.

CBS inferred they silenced the audio feed with static under direction by intelligence agencies. Keyhoe co-founded the National Investigations Committee on Aerial Phenomena (NICAP) in 1956 with Thomas Townsend Brown (antigravity researcher) that grew to 15,000 members. Keyhoe authored the book, The Flying Saucer Conspiracy, one of the first UFO books blaming the government for hiding information on Roswell and other UFO contacts or sightings.

"Donald Keyhoe." 2023. Wikipedia. April 12, 2023. https://en.wikipedia.org/wiki/Donald_Keyhoe.

Another interesting and surprising paradox you probably don't realize or maybe believe it or not. There has been direct concern by the Air Force Office of Special Investigations how much our government and US civilian population are alien hybrid clones. The Chinese may have cloned human hybrids under the guise of "gene edited babies."

The US may have DNA cloning of humans probably in some USAP, so the fact that an advanced civilization clones their own species or human subspecies is possible and has been confirmed. I must wonder how much DNA manipulation has been accomplished recently given our current political direction in this country.

Interestingly, when UFO congressional hearings are held historically, the military intelligence agencies and the CIA makes sure whoever is testifying has never had access to any UFO/ET SAP (Special Access Programs) that hide the ET and UFO technology research projects and our own ARV programs.

This intentional diversion is critical so if those who testify are ever forced to have lie detector tests, they can honestly say they have no knowledge. That clandestine pea and shell sight of hand game is about to change at an unprecedented level and witnesses like Rick Doty and Bob Lazar with proven track records that other government employees at Area 51 can testify. I have had that directly happen to me at the state level of government with the State of Tennessee regarding the political cosmetology fraud in our nation as laid out in my book, *Death By Pedicure*.

Greely, Henry T. 2020. "Cloning Humans Is Technically Possible. It's Curious No One Has Tried." STAT. February 21, 2020. https://www.statnews.com/2020/02/21/human-reproductive-cloning-curious-incident-of-the-dog-in-the-night-time/.

BBC. 2019. "China Jails 'Gene-Edited Babies' Scientist for Three Years." BBC News, December 30, 2019. https://www.bbc.com/news/world-asia-china-50944461.

The Government knows now that they can no longer keep a lid on this, and they are trying to save face about the ET/UFO factual evidence for disclosure that knocks on their false flag operations. The USAP protection for cloak and dagger operations are washing away quickly like a kid's sandcastle with the inevitable advancing tide. Even skeptics see the writing on the wall every time a military video from other nations becomes public.

The two paths the government must shed the eventual disdain is, 1. release the AG technology to a subcontractor like Lockheed Martin or Boeing with the ruse the subcontractor developed the antigravity (AG) technology independently decades ago and is just now admitting it. Any military contractor would be eager to be the corporate fall boy to access billions or trillions in subcontracts to spread over the rest of the aerospace industry. The military could also, 2. push the narrative the military itself developed/acquired AG just recently and play that public abstract for another 70 years like they have already since 1947.

Either way, it avoids the public embarrassment of the government hoarding the AG technology for so long. The same as Project Blue Book, Project Grudge, The Condon Report and Project Signs accumulated a 20-million-dollar project total budget cost to obscure the truth during the 50s, 60s, and 70s. An account of Project Blue Book was exposed by Hynek in his book UFO book, The UFO Experience: and another view of it was discussed by the project manager, Major Hector Quintanilla USAF in his unpublished book.

The US Government is afraid to tell the real story. The US military agencies and various intelligence governments agencies are afraid of our competing enemies who will use this UFO technology against us and invade our borders with no ability to stop them. That issue is sadly laughable as we don't need to worry about borders because our other civilian government via President Biden encourages hundreds of thousands illegal aliens and children with or without escorts, drug cartel gang members, foreign Interpol known criminals and terrorists to cross our border daily. That is the truth beyond question, and we don't need a Ministry of Truth to assure us differently.

Lt. Col Hector Quintanilla. 1974. UFO's: An Air Force Dilemma. Internet Archive. https://archive.org/details/ufos-an-air-force-dilemma/page/n5/mode/2up.

Our current leaders meet all these illegal aliens with a bottle of water, a pass to anywhere in the US and trillions in US TAXPAYER benefits. It is an embarrassment to those immigrants who came to our country legally and honestly followed the route to US citizenship. Who is going to protect us from the illegal alien ET immigrants and the aggressive ET alien species who may mean us harm? Gratefully there are friendly aliens like the EBENS who make up for the difference.

If you don't believe the UFO/ET phenomenon, then you need to OPEN YOUR EYES a bit wider. The proof is beyond question that I refer to in this book. There are tangible bits of alien wreckage, nano implants surgically removed by Dr. Lier in California (now deceased), FAA radar data and logs, volumes of military data, off earth products confirmed by Russia and our military retirees and hundreds of thousands of visual forms of proof is out there. (Earthfiles.com. SiriusDisclosure.com and GAIA.com)

My proof comes from a hundred books that I have read, interviews, GAIA TV show episodes and documentaries by credible journalists, witnesses, and hundreds of highly credible professional experts on every subject of science and history you can possibly find as well as my personal interviews with those who are beyond question.

Finally, after years of being forced to remain silent by the intensive military branches of our government, our government now wants the college professors and the media they previously muzzled to come forth with the "hidden evidence" to get our government off the hook.

Our government wants to deflect the generations of enormous public wrath that is now at the trigger of a momentous spring of the political mouse trap. The impending ridicule and embarrassment that the government used for 70 years on the same public and government individual whistleblowers they wanted to keep quiet is knocking at the front of their funding door. The military probably just ran out of hush money that AFOSI and CIA agents handed out like plastic money coins in children's board games for the last 70 years.

Now that disclosure has officially started like a slow mini drip on an IV bag, the new generations of blood hound journalists will pick up the scent of deceit and the trail will eventually backtrack to their media mentors who were complicit in their own program of accepting and obtaining bribes of political capital and cash that is drying up.

If you just love and trust our government 100% or are highly religious, this may make you label this book a tool of the devil, the cry of the antichrist or a real live horror story. But really this is a book of historical facts that many people will interpret personally that suit their religious upbringings, political convictions, or their internal media truth meters. You must decide what is real or fiction, then ACT accordingly.

CHAPTER 7:
VARIOUS PERSPECTIVES ON ETS AND UFOS

The discourse surrounding UFOs and extraterrestrials is one of diverse voices and perspectives, each contributing unique insights into the cosmic enigma that unfurls above us. Let's delve into four of these voices:

1. The first perspective comes from Tucker, my 9-year-old grandson. A curious observer, Tucker experienced the unexplainable during a UFO-watching tour in Sedona, Arizona. Our subsequent visit to Area 51 deepened this mystery, with our equipment picking up strange, inexplicable readings.

2. The second source of insight is the Fu Fu, a fictional entity crafted to deliver truth from an unexpected angle. The Fu Fu proposes an extraordinary theory: that ETs transported early humans and other species to Earth and have been tinkering with human DNA ever since. Surprisingly, the Fu Fu's wisdom seems to outpace even that of the US government.

3. The US government provides a third perspective, although not always a reliable one. For seven decades, they've woven a tapestry of deceit and misinformation about UFOs and ETs. Their motives are manifold - to save face, safeguard classified programs, and retain control over advanced technologies. While they're inching towards disclosure, it is likely they will continue their tactics of misinformation.

4. Lastly, we have the skeptics. These individuals often write off UFO sightings and ET encounters as nothing more than mirages, natural phenomena, or conventional objects like airplanes and balloons. However, their explanations often lack consistency and logic.

A wealth of evidence suggests that UFOs and ETs are real and have been interacting with Earth. Despite the US government's long-standing efforts to obscure this reality through misinformation and clandestine programs, the truth is beginning to surface through witness testimonies, recorded footage, and whistleblower revelations.

Using these voices to explore the questions that will be posed in this book serves as a conduit to explore these diverse viewpoints. The narratives are carefully crafted to encourage our young readers to question, evaluate, and form their own perspectives on these cosmic mysteries. The goal is not just to challenge the government's narrative, but to stimulate a hunger for truth and, ultimately, to foster a generation that will demand full disclosure.

CHAPTER 8
25 QUESTIONS ABOUT THE CHARACTERISTICS OF ETS

QUESTION 1:
The first question that often arises when we turn our gaze to the cosmos is: "Are there Star Beings, ETs, UFOs, or other non-human species that have visited Earth? Did Roswell really happen?" Let's examine this question from our four perspectives:

Tucker's Perspective:
"Yes, they exist!" exclaims Tucker, my grandson. I've taken him to Sedona to witness the night skies teeming with unexplained celestial phenomena, and to Area 51, where our instruments picked up strange signals. As an avid viewer of shows like 'Ancient Aliens,' Tucker believes in the long-standing presence of aliens on Earth. His conviction is mirrored in the drawings he contributes to our shared project - the book we're co-authoring.

The Fu Fu's Perspective:
The Fu Fu confidently affirms, "ETs are here now." It suggests that a diverse congregation of ETs, Star Beings, and non-human visitors, including humanoid hybrids, populated Earth long before modern humans. This intergalactic gathering has been unfolding for millions, perhaps billions of years, predating human existence on this planet.

The Fu Fu dismisses the promises of SETI, NASA, and 'Ivy League' astronomers about imminent contact, pointing instead to astrophysicists who have been working with ETs for seven decades. It proposes that with the testimony of these experts and government employees who've personally interacted with ETs and reverse-engineered their antigravity technology, we could establish interstellar communication.

Using Roswell as an example, the Fu Fu argues that the initial report of a 'Flying Saucer' capture was indeed accurate. Everything that followed, it claims, was a cover-up - "The Greatest Truth Never Told." The Fu Fu discredits the subsequent 'weather balloon' narrative and underscores the credibility of first-hand witnesses like Major Jesse Marcel Jr., who saw the actual Roswell wreckage as a child. For more insights, the Fu Fu recommends examining the testimonies of government officials like Richard Doty AFOSI, retired, who offer a detailed account of Roswell's true story. Over 600 witnesses have come forward to corroborate the crash, some presenting debris that the air force failed to collect. All witnesses and their families were threatened with death for most and promises of financial ruin for others. If any modern-day reparations should be given, all government silenced witnesses should be able to file claims.

AI Generated art of alien being taken captive / Leaked photo of "skinny bob"

Richard Doty while working for Hal Puthoff in his Austin, Texas research lab interviewed a 90 year old scientist in Fl during the 1990's whose name was still in the official Air force log of on-scene Roswell authorized personnel in 1947. The 90 year old scientist presented a thin 1 inch by 18-inch metal to Doty that folds and bends under heavy pressure but automatically reshapes itself with tremendous resilience you could not tear, rip, make a mark or scratch as described by Jesse Marcel in 1947. Doty also authenticates a 32-minute original 1947 video of the Roswell alien craft crash site with alien bodies filmed by an Army photographer Lt that was edited down to 17 minutes for the current 2023 Congressional closed-door hearings to watch and realize Roswell was true.

The Fu Fu acknowledges the countless American heroes and experts worldwide who've risked their lives and reputations to disclose their experiences with ETs and ET technology. The Fu Fu asserts that this wealth of information invites us to reconsider our understanding of our place in the cosmos.

The US Government's Perspective:

The official narrative often attributes UFO sightings to misidentified weather balloons, crash dummies, or mirages (USAF Project Blue Book).

The Skeptic's Corner:

Skeptics dismiss the existence of ETs and UFOs as debunked myths and fables. They argue that such beliefs are baseless and irrational.

Lastly, to those who quip, "I'll believe in UFOs when they land on the White House lawn," the Fu Fu would remind them that such an event already occurred in 1952, with UFOs observed over Washington for two consecutive weekends. These sightings were confirmed by radar, and the US Air Force even scrambled jets in response.

QUESTION 2:
What's the mode of transportation for extraterrestrials and the duration of their journey?

Tucker's Perspective:

As per Grand Bob, their voyage is faster than the speed of light.

The Fu Fu's Perspective:

Our archaic understanding of propulsion physics is primarily rooted in Albert Einstein's assertion that nothing can outpace light. This has led to the presumption that journeying to the nearest star could take centuries or even millennia. However, insights from our celestial neighbors, disclosed by Richard Doty, suggest that quantum speeds can be a hundredfold faster than the current known speed of light. Interstellar travel over 39 light years can be accomplished in 9 months via wormholes, blackholes and portals.

A supposed top-secret undertaking named Project Serpo involved an extraterrestrial exchange program where 12 of our astronauts embarked on a nine-month journey to planet Serpo, located 39 light years away, in 1965. This story was given a cinematic rendition in the Hollywood blockbuster, Close Encounters of the Third Kind. Whether you accept this as truth or fiction, it's intriguing.

AI Generated art of downed alien spacecraft by Russian MIG

Eight astronauts returned in 1978, spending the subsequent seven years in seclusion at an army AFB near Leavenworth as part of an agreement to keep this program confidential. This implies that through black holes, wormholes, and portals, travel distances can be hundreds of times faster than light, an astounding prospect. President Ronald Reagan was privy to this classified initiative, known as Project Serpo or "Project Crystal Knight," corroborated by the transcript of his meeting with the CIA Head in the book, The Secret Journey to Planet Serpo.

Here's an intriguing comparison between the social structures of the EBENs and Earth:

Our astronauts spent over a decade detailing their experiences, revealing some unique facts about the EBENs. Planet Serpo, a third smaller than Earth, had a controlled population of 500,000 to manage resources. The EBENs had undergone wars with the GREYs and other alien species to avert their occupation. They only allowed alien races on diplomatic missions, similar to our astronauts. Their planet was generally warmer due to the presence of two suns, one of which was a red sun, illuminating their 36-hour days.

The EBENs lived in a collective caste system, providing all essentials from a community store free of charge. Their diet primarily consisted of grain plant food, and they had mass agriculture, science/cloning, and manufacturing facilities centrally located. They held mass spiritual meetings daily and had a small security team to handle the almost non-existent crime rate.

The book, The Secret Journey to Planet Serpo, provides a riveting account of this story, corroborated by Richard Doty, an OSI agent, interviewed on GAIA TV. He presents hundreds of credible interviews with experts who have had direct, lifelong experiences with extraterrestrials.

The US Government's Perspective:
"Swamp gas is responsible for most UFO sightings" (Dr Hynek, Project Blue Book)

AI Generated depiction of UFOs over US capital

The Skeptic's Corner:
The FBI has dismissed all UFO theories as "bogus."

QUESTION 3:
What's the diversity of extraterrestrial species?

Tucker's Perspective:
There are multiple types out there.

The Fu Fu's Perspective:
As per Richard Doty, the military has identified five distinct alien species. However, researchers like Linda Moulton Howe and others propose a broader spectrum with 57 known subspecies, grouped into five main categories: EBENs, Grays, Quantaloids (Reptilian/Draconians), Trantaloids (Insectoids), Hepaloids, and Humanoids of Nordic and Tall Whites.

The US Government's Perspective:
There are no such entities like Bigfoot in the US or elsewhere in the world.

The Skeptic's Corner:
Need we repeat? There are no aliens.

From left to right, grey alien, Reptilian Alien, Trantaloid, Nordic Alien, Tall White Alien masquerading as Men in Black, Roswell Alien or EBEN

QUESTION 4:
How long is the lifespan of extraterrestrials?

AI Generated art of an elderly alien in a wheelchair

Tucker's Perspective:
According to Grand Bob, some alien species can live up to 700 years.

The Fu Fu's Perspective:
As per the Tall Whites, some aliens can live up to a staggering ten times the human lifespan, or around 700 years. This means that the juvenile stage for Tall White children can extend beyond 70 human years. The lifespan of other species varies, with the Tall Whites growing taller, up to ten feet, as they age, but also becoming increasingly frail, necessitating assistance for mobility past a certain point. The Greys, another species, have an average lifespan of 200-300 years (refer to the 'Millennial Hospitality' book series). William Tompkins, a TRW engineer, and researcher, claims that Nordics have lifespans between 1400-2300 years (see Gaia.com TV about the life of William Tompkins by Dr. Robert Woods: Season 11 episode 5).

In terms of color preferences, the Tall Whites reportedly appreciate a wide range of colors, similar to human tastes. However, most other ET species have not indicated specific color preferences. Recovered alien crafts are typically grey or brushed aluminum in color. An interesting note: a certain jellyfish species, Turritopsis nutricula, is virtually immortal, having the unique ability to revert from adult stage back to the polyp stage, an ability unrivaled in the animal kingdom.

The US Government's Perspective:
We appreciate the vibrant colors of our flag, red, white, and blue, but there's no evidence of extraterrestrial life. And to quote Franklin Roosevelt, during the build-up to World War II, "your boys are not going to be sent into any foreign wars."

The Skeptic's Corner:
The longest recorded human lifespan is 122 years, as demonstrated by Jeanne Calment, who lived in Arles, France.

QUESTION 5:
What is the physical appearance and anatomy of extraterrestrials, specifically their skin color and structure of hands and feet?

Tucker's Perspective:
They're typically long and skinny, with some digits missing.

The Fu Fu's Perspective:
The skin color of most reported alien species tends to be grey, with variations ranging from white-grey, orange-tinted, grey-blue to yellow-orange. The Reptilians are generally reported as green-grey. According to medical examinations conducted on retrieved crash victims, it's found that many alien species possess a single organ that combines the functionalities of heart and lungs. A common feature across different extraterrestrial species is the presence of long fingers, with certain species lacking fingernails while others have long ones.

Robine, J. 1998. "The Oldest Human." Science 279 (5358): 1831h1831. https://doi.org/10.1126/science.279.5358.1831h.

The number of digits in various alien races varies, typically between three to five, with many having three fingers and a thumb. Some even have features resembling suction cups akin to tree frogs. Reports indicate that unlike the 26 bones in a human foot, some extraterrestrial races have only three to five.

During autopsies of aliens, depending on the species, a strong unpleasant odor is often noted, particularly from their organ systems. Such was the case during the Roswell incident, where medical staff had to leave the autopsy area several times due to the strength of the smell.

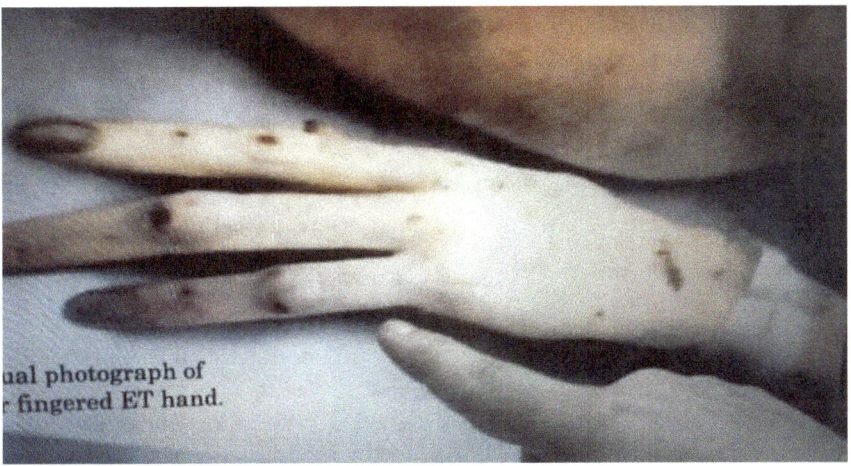

Archival photograph of UT hand

There have also been incidents where certain deceased aliens have released toxic gas upon death or autopsy. Some retrieval teams have reportedly died during capture or intentional extermination of aggressive alien species, particularly Trantaloids, from various containment facilities, such as Alpha Site 5 near the Area 51's S4 facility.

The Nordics grays and reptilians and Insectoids can all shape shift to look like normal humans.

The US Government's Perspective:
High-quality, orange plastic sandals are routinely provided to federal inmates.

The Skeptic's Corner:
An alien hand? Surely, you jest. There's no such thing.

QUESTION 6:
What is the dietary behavior of extraterrestrials?

Tucker's Perspective:
Yes, they eat.

The Fu Fu's Perspective:
The majority of ETs reportedly consume plant-based food and grains. An incident reported in Eagle River, Wisconsin on April 18, 1961, involved a UFO landing near a chicken farmer's (Joe Simonton, pictured below) property. The ETs requested water and reciprocated with a thin, waffle-like food item. Simonton tasted the extraterrestrial food, describing it as tasteless, reminiscent of cardboard, leading him to sympathize with the small stature of the ETs.

The head of the USAF's Project Bluebook confirmed that a sample of Simonton's received food was analyzed to be pure buckwheat pancakes. Richard Doty stated that the EBEN visitor, known as EBE1, carried food pellets on his craft, which would melt in the mouth when eaten. However, when human scientists attempted to consume these pellets, they didn't melt, presumably due to the lack of necessary enzymes in our saliva. Interestingly, one scientist from Los Alamos reported that EBENs seemed to prefer strawberry ice cream.

Greg. 2016. "The 1961 Story about a Chicken Farmer Who Claimed That Aliens Gave Him Pancakes." The Daily Grail. March 1, 2016. https://www.dailygrail.com/2016/03/the-1961-story-about-a-chicken-farmer-who-claimed-that-aliens-gave-him-pancakes/.

"UFO Sighting the Joe Simonton Story." n.d. Www.youtube.com. Accessed June 6, 2023. https://youtu.be/9oaXRQ9zAas.

When EBE1 exhausted his food pellet supply, he appeared to subsist on terrestrial vegetables, suggesting that ETs do consume water, as do all living organisms, except for hybrid Greys. There is no concrete evidence whether extraterrestrials enjoy popular Earth foods like Reese's Pieces. EBE1's death in 1952 remains a mystery, but his collaboration yielded significant anti-gravity technology insights.

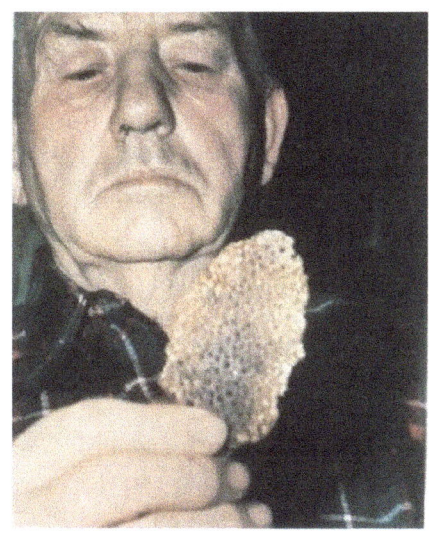

As per Richard Doty, some ET species, such as the insectoid Trantaloids, can produce their own food internally via organogenesis, similar to bacteria like Euglenas that create food/energy through internal chloroplasts. These species extract and consume golf-ball-sized pellets from their hip region, but they also drink water. Certain insectoid species consume meat similar to humans.

The US Government's Perspective:
"I did not have 'blank' relations with that woman" (President Bill Clinton, January 26, 1998)

The Skeptic's Corner:
Aliens don't exist, so why worry about their dietary habits?

QUESTION 7:
Are certain extraterrestrial races considered dangerous or more prone to causing harm or abduction?

Tucker's Perspective:
Yes, Grand Bob warns about certain aggressive insectoid and reptilian races.

"Eben Pilots of Roswell." n.d. Gaia. Accessed June 6, 2023. https://www.gaia.com/video/eben-pilots-roswell.

The Fu Fu's Perspective:

There are three species from Zeta Reticuli, namely the EBENs (a variant of the Greys), the Quadloids, (Insectoids and reptilians) and the Trantaloids other insectoids, Heplaloids (multi segmented insect bodies), and Archquloids (humanoids with large, curved noses like depicted by Egyptian pyramid drawings) from the Cygnus star system near the great rift also exist.

The Tall Whites cooperate with humans and share basic technologies, however, proximity to them, especially their offspring, can result in lethal retaliation. The Quadloids or Reptilians have a notorious history of aggressive abductions and distressing human examinations. Certain Greys utilize their grey hybrid servants to carry out emotionless examinations on paralyzed humans, exhibiting a cold, detached demeanor.

The EBENs, a more compassionate version of the Greys, have fewer connections with abductions. The most dangerous are the Trantaloids, a type of aggressive insectoid (distinct from praying mantis-like insectoids), known for their intolerance of other alien species or humanoids, and their invasion-driven mindset. They also possess the ability to mimic the body types of Tall Whites or Nordics. Efforts to eradicate these Trantaloids are being made by the Galactic Federation of ETs. Our military Alien control teams have previously captured some of these beings. Although not always cooperative or communicative in custody, some have died during their imprisonment.

(Richard Doty on Gaia interviews detailed two alien insectoid escapes from area 51. One escape involving a Quadloid resulted in the killing of a father who was camping with his family at Silver Bow NV. The mother drove from the area with her two children. A military police officer found and shot the alien insect in the head ending the escape. The mother filed claims against the AF and was eventually told what happened and the AF financially settled and took care of her family.

Doty related another escaped Trantaloid resulted in capturing the alien insectoid by a wildlife trapper in the area north of area 51 and north of Tonopah Missile range. Several law enforcement agencies including the NYE county Sheriff department and the Nevada State Police were involved. Doty suggested that some of the insectoids have reversed knees and can run at tremendous speed of 20-30 mph.

The US Government's Perspective:

Former President Obama, during a talk show interview about UFOs, commented, "I can't tell you on air i.e., I am not supposed to talk about it."

The Skeptic's Corner:

"Trust me, the US government has the Border Secure." (Joe Biden, 2022)

"Barack Obama: 'When It Comes to Aliens, There Are Things I Just Can't Tell You on Air.'" N.d. Futurism. Accessed June 6, 2023. https://futurism.com/barack-obama-aliens.

QUESTION 8:

Do we have extraterrestrials that are presently accommodated here on Earth or maintain bases on Earth?

Tucker's Perspective:

Yes, Grand Bob has always said that Earth has served as a Galactic Hotel for ETs for hundreds of millions of years.

The Fu Fu's Perspective:

Currently, we have approximately several hundred ETs on Earth at any given time. These visitors primarily stay at a spaceport near Area 51 territory, known as Area 54, which houses a permanent base for the Tall Whites.

The United States Air Force extends hospitality to the Tall Whites, Nordics, and formerly the Greys, at Cheech Air Force Base near Area 51 on the Nellis Air Force Testing Range. The EBENS were accommodated by Los Alamos National Laboratory from 1948 to 1952. (As per Richard Doty's interviews on GAIA TV and Charles Hall's book series, "Millennium Hospitality.")

All United Nations member nations have signed a treaty to jointly oversee Antarctica, with the agreement that no aircraft are to fly over the North or South poles. It's reported that aliens have bases under the sea in every ocean on Earth. During WWII, the Germans allegedly collaborated with the Nordics and Reptilians to design UFOs for operational use. ET bases are thought to be scattered in mountainous areas, underground caverns, and virtually any environment on earth. (Ancient Aliens). Several other USAF Bases in the continental US have hosted ETs such as Dugway AFB, Kirtland AFB and most recently, the very remote AFB at the Johnston Atoll base in the pacific southwest of Hawaii.

Richard Doty mentions several locations where we "hold" hostile aliens, one being Area 51 at Alpha Site 5 (A-S-5), near Site 4 (S4) where alien craft are held. In a highly classified operation called "Amber Sun", Doty was involved in the retrieval of an escaped alien from A-S-5. Details of his account can be found here.

Doty also related we have housed live aliens at Los Alamos and Sandia Labs from various crash sites and even assigned a USAF Captain to provide round the clock access to debrief the EBEN 1 alien for a two-year (1947-49) period of time on various ET technologies and exchange of language.

Doty also disclosed the discovery of a secret UFO base right in the middle of one of our own top-secret bases at the Tonopah missile ranges, which we handled in a "terminal manner" with a nuclear weapon.

Rumor has it that the Secretary of Defense recently visited Area 52 near the Tonopah Ranges, sparking speculation about possible disclosure.

The US Government's Perspective:
"Our borders are secure, and we have no mass migration into the US." (VP K. Harris, May 2022)

The Skeptic's Corner:
"Just because nearly 5 million illegal 'aliens' have crossed the 'Biden border' in 2021-2022 doesn't mean that any 'space' aliens are here."

Migrants heading to towards the US Border

"Secret E.T. Base Discovered!" n.d. Gaia. Accessed June 6, 2023. https://www.gaia.com/video/secret-et-base-discovered.

"US Secretary of Defense at Area 51?" n.d. Gaia. Accessed June 6, 2023. https://www.gaia.com/video/us-secretary-of-defense-at-area-51.

"Special Investigations Agent: Richard Doty." N.d. Gaia. Accessed June 6, 2023. https://www.gaia.com/video/special-investigations-agent-richard-doty?fullplayer=preview.

Contributor, Bethany Blankley | The Center Square. N.d. "Nearly 5 Million Foreign Nationals Have Entered the U.S. Illegally since Biden Took Office." The Center Square. https://www.thecentersquare.com/national/nearly-5-million-foreign-nationals-have-entered-the-u-s-illegally-since-biden-took-office/article_dfaa6376-1e25-11ed-b23d-77891ec8afbf.html.

QUESTION 9:

Do we possess alien energy systems that we've reverse-engineered?

Tucker's Perspective:

Yes, we've constructed UFOs.

AI generated art of a small 12 by 12 Plexiglas-like energy battery capable of running an entire town

The Fu Fu's Perspective:

We have been given technology by ETs that has allowed us to use Zero Point Energy devices that collect energy from our air or atmosphere we breath and provides unlimited power for any demand put up the load for any type of electrically run items. The Air Force recovery teams have found these alien developed plexiglass type small energy "unlimited battery devices" running large UFOs with extra units as backups for interstellar or antigravity travel.

The keys to our children's future regarding unlimited zero-point energy, antigravity propulsion and time travel exist in the vaults of Defense Intelligence Agencies and the US patent office under various secrecy blueprints. Over 6000 patents regarding limitless energy for manufacturing, residential power, and antigravity travel whether terrestrial or off-planet have been classified as top secret and will not be seen in our lifetimes due to the distribution of power and greed literally and figuratively. This will not change unless our legislators and the president are determined to share these with the public and private manufactures.

The US Government's Perspective:
"I am not a crook." (Richard Nixon, 1975)

The Skeptic's Corner:
Putin will never invade Ukraine and aliens aren't real.

QUESTION 10:
Do extraterrestrials sleep?

AI Generated art of alien sleeping quarters

Tucker's Perspective:
Some aliens do sleep, while others just rest.

The Fu Fu's Perspective:
Not all extraterrestrial beings require sleep as we understand it. Some, instead, take repose in uniquely designed relaxation spaces such as recessed calming benches built into walls, bunk beds, and tabletop systems, especially during prolonged journeys. Alien humanoid automatons, clones, or hybrids are typically programmed not to require sleep, though they do have periods of rest. Meanwhile, other humanoid extraterrestrials such as the Tall Whites, Nordics, and certain types of Greys do partake in sleep-like behavior.

The US Government's Perspective:
"Don't read it, just sign it." (Nancy Pelosi, regarding the 1000-page ACA bill)

The Skeptic's Corner:
Aliens don't need to sleep because they're not real.

QUESTION 11:
Do extraterrestrials reproduce?

AI Generated art of two aliens

"Why Putin Won't Invade Ukraine." 2022. Atlantic Council. February 16, 2022. https://www.atlanticcouncil.org/blogs/new-atlanticist/why-putin-wont-invade-ukraine/.

Tucker's Perspective:

I'm just 8, Grand Bob hasn't told me about that yet. He told me to ask my mother.

The Fu Fu's Perspective:

Reproduction among extraterrestrials varies widely. Some species utilize advanced genetic techniques, akin to lab-based DNA manipulation, while others, such as the EBENs, Nordics, and Tall Whites, reproduce in a manner similar to humans. However, it's noteworthy that certain species, like the Greys, have reportedly lost their ability to reproduce naturally and now rely on cloning or hybridization.

The US Government's Perspective:

Don't ask your parents, just talk to any drag queen

The Skeptic's Corner:

Aliens aren't real, thus the idea of them reproducing is debunked.

QUESTION 12:

<u>Do extraterrestrials express emotions like anger or laughter?</u>

AI Generated art of two aliens showing emotion

Tucker's Perspective:

Yes, some do.

The Fu Fu's Perspective:

Alien species are as diverse as their emotional capacity. Some extraterrestrials, especially genetically modified hybrids or humanoid robots are known to exhibit little to no emotional response. However, other species, such as the EBENs, some Greys, and the Tall Whites, are reputedly capable of displaying a range of emotions albeit limited in a human context. Interestingly, according to accounts like those detailed in the Millennium Hospitality series, the Tall Whites are known to exhibit a full range of emotions including humor, and sometimes use their superiority to intimidate humans for their amusement. It's also said that certain races, like the Reptilians and Insectoids, have a history of aggression. The Hollywood movie PAUL offers an engaging representation of friendly alien-human interactions. (Refer to Charles J. Hall's book, Millennial Hospitality for more information.)

The US Government's Perspective:
National Security Agency or NSA - "We do not record the public's cell phone calls."

The Skeptic's Corner:
The concept of aliens is a money-making scheme for Hollywood, targeting gullible audiences.

QUESTION 13:

Do extraterrestrials wear clothes and use currency?

Tucker's Perspective:
Yes.

The Fu Fu's Perspective:
Several extraterrestrial species, such as the Ebens, Greys, and Humans, Nordics, and Tall Whites have been reported to don uniquely fabricated garments akin to a thin exoskeleton that offers protection. When it comes to monetary systems, instead of conventional currency, advanced extraterrestrial civilizations often engage in resource exchange or bartering. Species like the EBENs operate on a system similar to communism, where everything is provided freely, while other civilizations such as the Greys and Nordics have an accomplishment-based credit system. (Refer to Richard Doty's interviews on GAIA and Earthfiles.com)

The US Government's Perspective:

There's no such thing as alien attire or currency. But there are Weapons of Mass Destruction.

The Skeptic's Corner:

Dressing up dolls to resemble aliens doesn't make them real. Aliens don't have bank accounts.

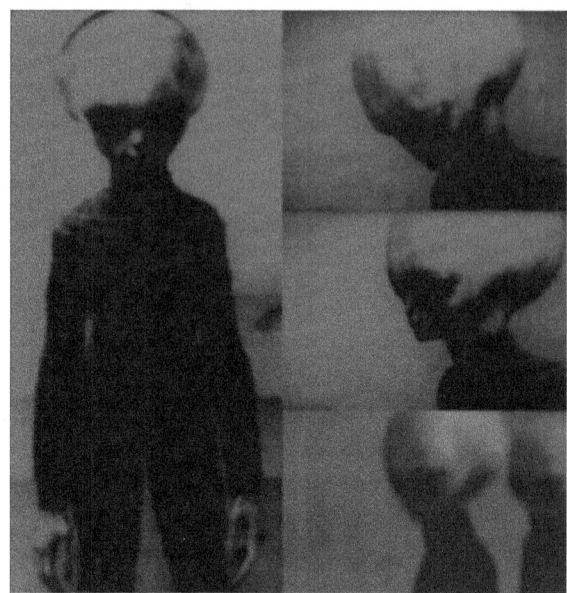

Archival photos of famous "Skinny Bob" alien

QUESTION 14:

Are extraterrestrials typically lean or robust?

Tucker's Perspective:
I think both. But I've only seen the picture of Skinny Bob.

The Fu Fu's Perspective:
Most extraterrestrial species are reported to have slender physiques, large heads proportional to their bodies, elongated limbs, and significantly larger eyes for low-light vision. Species such as the EBENs, the Greys, the Nordics, and the Tall Whites generally have slender bodies and predominantly vegetarian diets. However, the universe's vastness implies an enormous diversity of life forms, including the potential for heavier set extraterrestrials.

The US Government's Perspective:
The federal government doesn't use tax money for weight management programs for illegal aliens.

The Skeptic's Corner:
The concept of a weight watchers' program for obese aliens may be amusing, but it doesn't prove their existence.

QUESTION 15:

Do aliens levitate, and do they teach their young to pilot spacecraft?

Tucker's Perspective:

Yes, Grand Bob read a book that says they do.

AI generated art of 1950s era human flying saucer

The Fu Fu's Perspective:

According to Charles Hall, some Tall Whites utilize technology that allows them to levitate or travel approximately a foot above the ground. Other species can teleport or pass through walls. They do seem to take an active interest in their offspring's development, teaching them to fly spacecraft from a young age. It's speculated that the Roswell crash in 1947 was the result of young aliens piloting crafts recklessly, a behavior likened to Earth teenagers pulling pranks. When Earth astronauts visited the EBENs' home planet Serpo, they were forbidden from interacting with EBEN children.

The US Government's Perspective:
There are no extraterrestrial children in the White House bathrooms.

The Skeptic's Corner:
Believing in levitating aliens and George Jetson might require a reality check. (Refer to Biden's Ministry of Truth)

QUESTION 16:

Do ETs believe in a Supreme Power?

AI Generated art of a Christian church building with a tower and satellite dishes

Tucker's Perspective:
Yes.

The Fu Fu's Perspective:
Many extraterrestrial races such as the EBENs reportedly adhere to a belief system centered around a Supreme Being or power. They are purportedly spiritual beings, practicing meditation and prayer, and acknowledging the concept of a soul that persists as a form of consciousness post-mortem. Earth religions, like Catholicism, are beginning to consider the potential existence of extraterrestrial races. The book "Chariots of the Gods" by Erich Von

Däniken and the TV series "Ancient Aliens" suggest that the biblical term "angel" could be replaced with "ET" or "UFO", potentially demystifying our understanding of these divine entities. This interpretation supposes that shiny beings or flying chariots mentioned in religious texts could have been descriptions of extraterrestrials and their crafts. Hindu and Muslim religious texts also refer to celestial beings and crafts that could be construed as extraterrestrials or UFOs.

The US Government's Perspective:
"In God We Trust" - an accompanying image of a UFO with the same slogan.

The Skeptic's Corner:
Skeptic's Corner: Concrete proof of a supreme deity or divine entity still eludes us.

QUESTION 17:

Have there been military conflicts with extraterrestrials?

Tucker's Perspective:
Yes.

The Fu Fu's Perspective:
Reports suggest there have been several confrontations between humans and extraterrestrials. One case involves Richard Doty, an OSI agent, who allegedly discovered and subsequently destroyed a covert UFO base within the Unita Mountains on the Tonopah missile range. This reportedly led to a swift retaliation by the extraterrestrials, who targeted an underground complex at Boiling AFB near Washington, DC, resulting in a brutal attack on high-ranking officers and command staff. Other historical instances of conflict include Admiral Byrd's 1947 Operation High Jump, a secret mission to Antarctica that was met with resistance from unidentified flying objects. An engineer named Paul Schneider claims to have survived a subterranean altercation with Grey aliens at Dulce, NM, that cost the lives of over 60 government agents and military personnel. Reports also indicate various encounters between US river patrol boats and UFOs during the Vietnam War, and a documented UFO presence over Washington, DC, in 1952 led to an aerial skirmish with US fighter jets. It's suggested that these skirmishes have resulted in both human and extraterrestrial casualties.

The US Government's Perspective:
Biden says has seen the man in the moon.

The Skeptic's Corner:
If the existence of extraterrestrials isn't confirmed, it stands to reason that no wars could have occurred with them.

QUESTION 18:
Can we enhance longevity, cure diseases like cancer, and address global health concerns using advanced alien technology and DNA science?

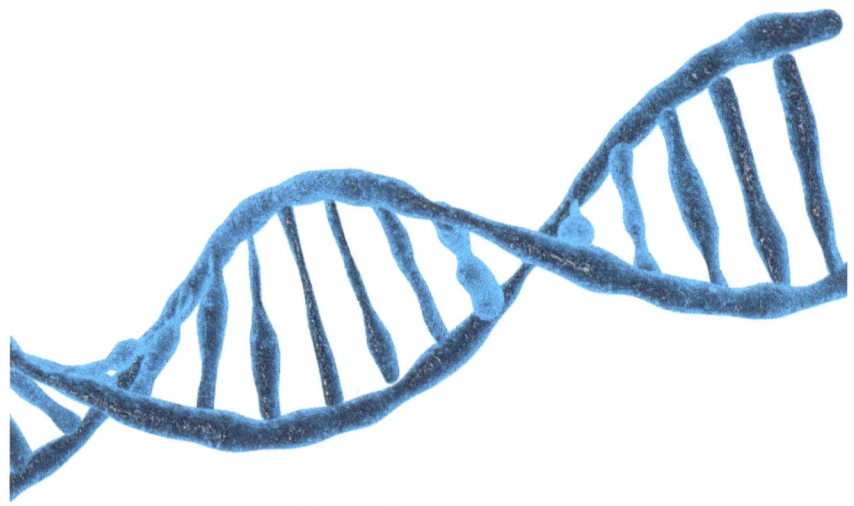

Tucker's Perspective:
For an expert opinion, consult Grand Bob, but, "Yes, I believe so".

The Fu Fu's Perspective:
Undoubtedly, humans have already reaped the benefits of alien technologies, manifesting in advancements like lasers, fiber optics, and computer chip designs. Extraterrestrials have reportedly been toying with the human genetic code for millions of years.

Washington, District of Columbia 1800 I. Street NW, and Dc 20006. n.d. "PolitiFact - That Video of President Joe Biden Discussing Aliens Is so Far out It's Fake." @Politifact. Accessed June 14, 2023. https://www.politifact.com/factchecks/2023/feb/28/facebook-posts/that-video-of-president-joe-biden-discussing-alien/

Techniques such as CRISPR gene editing and gene therapy, considered to be advancements in our DNA manipulation capabilities, have already provided cures for numerous cancers and genetic disorders. ETs have supposedly utilized DNA splicing to enhance their own species and others. The Turritopsis nutricula, a nearly immortal jellyfish species, serves as an interesting case study for researchers. Its unique DNA process is being investigated by pharmaceutical companies to potentially reverse the aging process, effectively achieving immortality.

The US Government's Perspective:

We would like to address the narratives that have been circulating since May 18th, 2023, regarding Dr. Garry Nolan. Dr. Nolan, a Stanford Pathologist Professor, immunologist, and DNA researcher of significant repute, was allegedly contracted by the Defense Intelligence Agency (DIA) for an intriguing task.

He was said to have been examining 'metamaterials' believed to have originated from other planets, and supposedly reviewing MRIs from American pilots, who have reportedly been piloting reverse-engineered UFOs or ARVs. This has led to a surge in speculation and, dare I say, an onslaught of imaginative conjecture.

The Skeptic's Corner:

Yes, and now we're supposed to believe that Dr. Nolan is fully convinced about the existence of extraterrestrials among us. I mean, come on, the man who built a solid career in pathology and immunology suddenly decides to wear the hat of a government whistleblower revealing so-called 'hidden truths' about aliens.

"The Immortal Jellyfish Lives up to Its Name." 2019. Ocean Conservancy. July 1, 2019. https://oceanconservancy.org/blog/2019/07/01/immortal-jellyfish-lives-name/.

"'100%' Aliens Have Already Arrived -Dr. Garry Nolan | SALT IConnections New York." n.d. Www.youtube.com. Accessed June 7, 2023. https://www.youtube.com/watch?v=e2DqdOw6Uy4.

"Joe Biden 'Has to Be Taken out of Circulation' after 'Rambling about Men on the Moon.'" N.d. Www.youtube.com. Accessed June 7, 2023. https://www.youtube.com/watch?v=JLVNYNEXr_c.

QUESTION 19:

Could ET races be taking on human forms, modifying their skin types, colors, and textures to seamlessly blend into our society and study our civilization without revealing their alien identities?

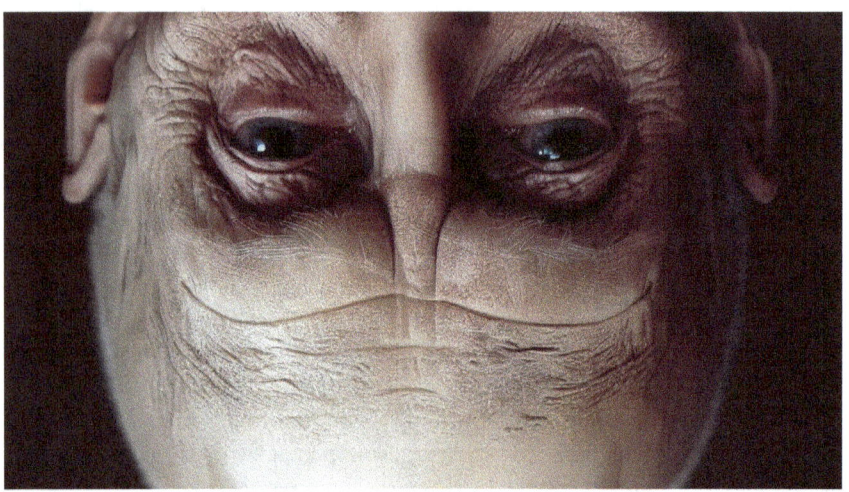

AI Generated art of upside-down face looking alien

Tucker's Perspective:

Grand Bob once allowed me to watch a TV show called "Ancient Aliens," which suggested that aliens are among us.

The Fu Fu's Perspective:

It's true that five major alien body types have been identified, with many ETs reported to create humanoid robots, i.e., hybrids or clones, for various purposes like exploration, manufacturing, and menial tasks.

Supposedly, military, and associated subcontractors have devised DNA tests to ascertain if suspected aliens are integrating into our society. There have been claims, such as the one involving an Air Force captain in Washington, DC, of aliens living among us. The captain was allegedly never seen sleeping and rarely eating, consuming only water, and while outwardly normal, he exhibited peculiarities in his eyes and a consistently calm demeanor.

"Contact: Who Is Here and Why." N.d. Gaia. Accessed June 7, 2023. https://www.gaia.com/video/contact-who-here-and-why.

The US Government's Perspective:

In a recent development, the Biden administration's "Ministry of Truth" or the Department of Homeland Security has established the Disinformation Governance Board (DGB). According to Politico, this board's mission is to counter misinformation related to homeland security, with a focus on irregular migration and Russia—a twist seemingly more surreal than fiction.

The Skeptic's Corner:

The notion of aliens morphing into humans may prompt some, including President Biden, to exclaim, "Come On Man…. Aliens Turning into Humans? Let me give you a hug." (Biden Science)

QUESTION 20:

Is it possible for humans to learn meditation techniques that allow them to communicate or establish contact with extraterrestrial beings (ETs) through telepathy?

Tucker's Perspective:

According to Grand Bob, the answer is yes. I think I saw that on "Ancient Aliens."

"Contact: Who Is Here and Why." N.d. Gaia. https://www.gaia.com/video/contact-who-here-and-why.

The Fu Fu's Perspective:

There are humans who have a natural ability to concentrate through meditation and prayer to the point where they can perform telekinesis (using the mind to move objects without touch), telepathy (communicating mentally without vocalization), and remote viewing.

Technically, anyone can learn to meditate using various methods, which could potentially enable them to concentrate intensely enough to create conditions in the brain that facilitate the use of these skills, including communication with ETs. The idea is that once you can reach out to ETs, you may increase their receptivity to establishing contact. It seems that some individuals are naturally more adept at mastering these skills.

Several ufologists and experts claim to have communicated with ETs during contact events. Dr. Steven Greer, one of the most active ufologists, offers this CE5 training through www.sirusdisclosure.com. The SETI group in Washington state has allegedly used remote viewing to observe ET activity on Earth and other planets.

It's important to note, however, that there are certain alien species who do not permit contact with humans and have no interest in establishing such relationships. Species like the Trantaloids and Arachnoids are said to have this disposition because they seek to dominate other species and don't wish to be influenced by humans.

To achieve these telepathic feats, you must find a balance between beta waves and theta and delta waves. ECETI in Washington State asserts that most people can learn or be trained to develop telepathic abilities or become remote viewers with practice.

"E.T. Communication & Contact." N.d. Gaia. Accessed June 7, 2023. https://www.gaia.com/video/et-communication-contact.

"Portals & Protocols of et Contact." N.d. Gaia. Accessed June 7, 2023. https://www.gaia.com/video/portals-protocols-of-et-contact.

"My Night Hunting UFOs at an Alien Ranch." N.d. Thrillist. Accessed June 7, 2023. https://www.thrillist.com/travel/nation/eceti-ranch-trout-lake-washington-ufos.

Mishlove, Jeffrey. 2018. "Remote Viewing of UFOs and Other Mysteries with Paul H. Smith." YouTube. https://www.youtube.com/watch?v=CwPi8RzeIC8.

"Remote Viewing." 2021. Wikipedia. November 11, 2021. https://en.wikipedia.org/wiki/Remote_viewing.

The US Government's Perspective:

As President Ford candidly put it, he proposed that "Congress investigate the rash of reported sightings of unidentified flying objects in Southern Michigan and other parts of the country." His attached news release stated that he was unsatisfied with the Air Force's explanation of these sightings and criticized astrophysicist J. Allen Hynek's "swamp gas" theory as dismissive.

The Skeptic's Corner:

There are skeptics who might jest, "Come On Man… I talk to Aliens and little people in my closet every day," making light of such claims, as can be seen in this clip featuring a Joe Biden look-alike, or possibly Biden himself. Desert conferences for ET/UFO contact are a thing as well.

QUESTION 21:

Do alien species utilize robots to assist them?

Tucker's Perspective:

Yes.

The Fu Fu's Perspective:

Absolutely. Alien hybrids or clones are, in essence, biologically synthetic robots that extraterrestrial races utilize for space exploration, planetary reconnaissance, and mundane tasks. These hybrids are also designed to imitate human features, allowing them to blend in with our society for learning purposes as well as for risky missions that might endanger the pure alien species.

Lawrence, Kerri. 2018. "Do Records Show Proof of UFOs?" National Archives. February 8, 2018. https://www.archives.gov/news/articles/do-records-show-proof-of-ufos.

"Joe Biden Rambles: 'Whether or Not There's a Man on the Moon.'" N.d. GOP. Accessed June 7, 2023. https://gop.com/video/joe-biden-rambles-whether-or-not-theres-a-man-on-the-moon/.

Grey Aliens and the Harvesting of Souls. 2010. Www.simonandschuster.com. https://www.simonandschuster.com/books/Grey-Aliens-and-the-Harvesting-of-Souls/Nigel-Kerner/9781591431039.

The US Government's Perspective:

We have self-replicating nano robots, which are funded by DARPA (Defense Advanced Research Program Agency), a federal entity overseeing the development of technology for military use.

The Skeptic's Corner:

Skeptics might sigh, "We are getting pretty tired of debunking Aliens and UFOs all the time," their patience evidently wearing thin.

QUESTION 22:
Are extraterrestrial species equipped with space weapons?

Tucker's Perspective:

Yes.

The Fu Fu's Perspective:

The cosmos teems with a wide array of weapons systems, from hand-fired to shoulder-mounted. The EBENs deploy directed energy weapons (DEW), also recognized as scalar energy weapons. Like lasers, these personal defense weapons demonstrated their power at the Tonopah missile range, penetrating rock as deep as 50 feet at more than 100 feet from a target. A hole large enough to peer through was left in the mountainside.

The Tall Whites wield a device resembling a 6–7-inch white pencil capable of emitting a tunable multi-frequency beam. This hand weapon targets specific atoms within the human body, such as calcium, sodium, and iodine. Tuning the weapon to different frequencies can result in a range of effects, from mild shock to lethal pain. For example, targeting calcium can induce an immediate hypnotic sleep. Alarmingly, the weapon can be adjusted to force blood to leak from arteries, potentially causing the victim to bleed to death in just 2 minutes.

One unfortunate recipient of a near-lethal dose was Airman Charles J. Hall. According to his book series, "Millennium Hospitality," he was shot in the throat by a young alien female. His recovery was overseen solely by a tall white alien physician, the Air Force willing to let him perish to avoid disrupting their treaty with the Tall Whites and Greys.

CNN, Katie Hunt. n.d. "World's First Living Robots Can Now Reproduce, Scientists Say." CNN. https://www.cnn.com/2021/11/29/americas/xenobots-self-replicating-robots-scn/index.html.

As Hall's book reveals, high command staff at Nellis AFB has established intergalactic relations with the Tall White Nordics and the Greys, hosted near what is now known as Creech AFB. This site has been a vacation spot for these ETs for thousands of years.

Additionally, psychotronic weapons reportedly have the capability to manipulate brain waves, causing distress and even death. This technology has allegedly been used against US diplomats in Cuba and China.

The US Government's Perspective:

President Dwight D. Eisenhower, in his final presidential speech on January 17, 1961, warned of the military-industrial complex and the potential for the disastrous rise of misplaced power. He was subtly referring to the alien association with the military and their preparedness to use any means necessary to retain secrecy around alien technology.

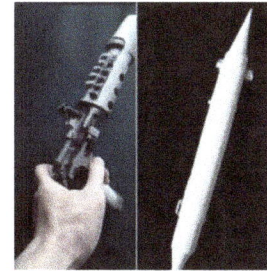

AI Generated art

Any patent applications related to antigravity, propulsion, communications, or energy are meticulously reviewed by every intelligence branch. Any agency can classify these patents as secret for up to 50 years, with little justification and no remuneration. Presently, over 6000 patents are held in such a status, as confirmed by Dr. Valone, a former 20-year patent examiner with top-secret clearance.

"Creech Air Force Base in Indian Springs, NV | MilitaryBases.com." n.d. Military Bases. Accessed June 7, 2023. https://militarybases.com/nevada/creech/.

Howe, Linda Moulton, and Dr Raymond W. Boeche. N.d. "September 10 2020 Revision Complete Record of DOD Contacts." Www.academia.edu. https://www.academia.edu/44080434/September_10_2020_Revision_Complete_Record_of_DOD_contacts.

admin. 2022. "Century of Suppressed Electrotherapy, Exotic Propulsion & Free Energy Technologies." Exopolitics. July 19, 2022. https://exopolitics.org/century-of-suppressed-exotic-technologies/.

The Skeptic's Corner:
There are no aliens, hence, no alien ray guns.

QUESTION 23:

Do extraterrestrials assess human reactions to their presence and do individuals who experience abductions or close encounters with UFOs suffer from mental gaps, time distortions, or psychological issues afterward?

Tucker's Perspective:
Yes, people who see real UFOs can blank out.

The Fu Fu's Perspective:
Absolutely. Diverse alien species continually scrutinize and evaluate humans for alterations in our behaviors, our acceptance of extraterrestrial beings, and shifts in our drive to develop, trial, and flaunt our nuclear arsenal to other nations. Experiencing time lapses is commonplace, with UFO encounters often inducing an instant hypnotic state, followed by slow recovery, lingering lethargy, headaches, and other symptoms of nausea.

These hypnotic frequencies are disseminated by UFOs and extraterrestrial entities, and various forms of aerosol gas can be employed to induce paralysis or amnesia-like conditions prior to abductions or aggressive actions. At times, frequency generators attuned to human frequencies can induce hypnotic trances.

The Barney and Betty Hill abduction event, widely recognized and often cited, has become a benchmark case in the study of alien abductions. The couple's story brought the term "alien abduction" into mainstream and tabloid vernacular and both reported loss of time.

The US Government's Perspective:
Officially, the government denies the existence of aliens, negating any psychological basis for testing humans for extraterrestrial DNA.

"The Zeta Reticuli (or Ridiculi) Incident | Astronomy Magazine." N.d. Astronomy.com. https://astronomy.com/bonus/zeta.

The Skeptic's Corner:

From our perspective, there are no aliens, thus, no reason to worry about ray guns or related phenomena.

QUESTION 24:

Are ETS truthful with Humans?

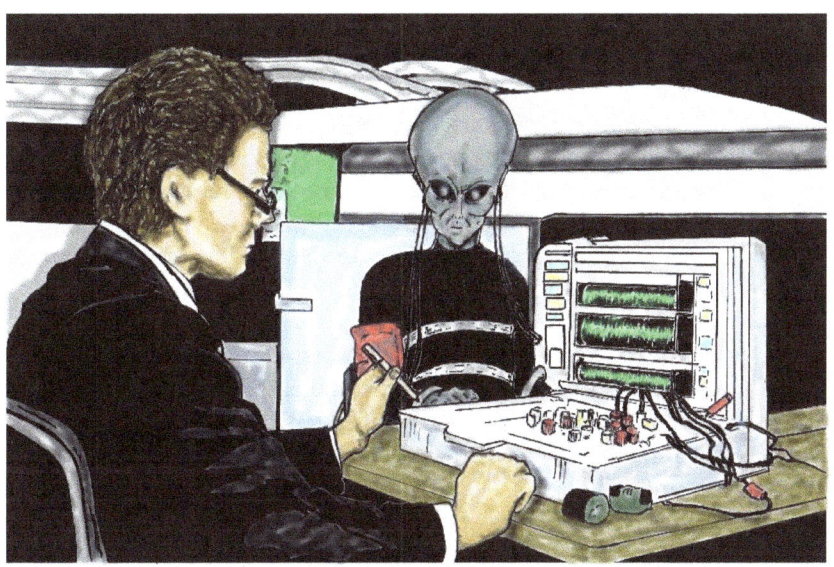

Tucker's Perspective:

Not always.

The Fu Fu's Perspective:

Treaties with aliens have been broken with reference to abductions of humans, animal mutilations and visitations in restricted military areas. We have had multiple alien races in captivity, and we have tried to debrief or interrogate these aliens to gain more insight into their technology in antigravity, weapons and time travel. Aliens have their own agendas when dealing with humans and not all of them are honest in nature.

The US Government's Perspective:

You can have any health policy you want just like congress, and it won't cancel.

The Skeptic's Corner:

Better believe us or we will make fun of you in as many articles that we can.

QUESTION 25:

Is there a "Yellow Book" that the EBEN race gave to us, containing a detailed account of their interactions with Earth over thousands of years?

Tucker's Perspective:

As Grand Bob says, "Yes, they did present us with a magical Yellow History Book."

The Fu Fu's Perspective:

Indeed, the EBENs bestowed upon us a holographic book. This account traces back 2300 years and stretches until 1970. The fascinating aspect of this book is its interactive nature: it can be read in any language the reader is most comfortable with. However, the catch is, if your gaze shifts away or you pause your reading, it reverts to the beginning. Therefore, it often takes several days for a reader to finish the book, depending on their endurance to stay awake and their understanding of navigating the Yellow Book.

The US Government's Perspective:

To quote any USAF Four Star General from the past 70 years, "There are no extraterrestrials on Earth, and we have no alien EBEN Yellow History Books accessible to the public in our local school libraries or the Library of Congress that we are aware of."

The Skeptic's Corner:

To borrow a phrase from President Biden, "Come On, Man….For the Last Time…Our Borders are Secure!"

CHAPTER 9
25 QUESTIONS ABOUT THE CHARACTERISTICS
OF UFOS

QUESTION 1:
Do we possess alternatives to traditional rocket propulsion for space travel, such as Alien Reproduction Vehicles (ARVs)?

AI Generated art of alien spacecraft

Tucker's Perspective:
Yes, UFOs are real; I personally witnessed them through military-grade night vision in Sedona AZ in May 2021.

The Fu Fu's Perspective:
With the recovery of alien crafts in 1947 and 1949, the US military pioneered basic anti-gravity technology in 1952. The survivors from these crafts, known as EBENs or Extraterrestrial Biological Entities, facilitated the development of super energy technologies and ARVs.

An estimated 50% of all UFO sightings (like the Tic Tacs) are, according to my estimates, US-made ARVs. Mark McCandlish and Brad Sorenson, highly skilled aerospace graphic artists, were invited to an airshow where ARVs "floating on electromagnetic waves" were on display at Norton AFB. Regrettably, Mark was unable to attend, but Brad witnessed three varying-sized levitating saucers. Together they created the first ARV blueprint based on their observations.

Contrary to popular belief, we achieved off-world travel via our ARV technology before the first NASA rocket in Oct. 11, 1958. Our NASA astronauts encountered aliens on their moon and Mars expeditions using conventional rockets. We also established bases on these celestial bodies, and even ventured to other moons and planets in our solar system with our reversed alien technology.

_____

"O Fantástico Relato de Bill Uhouse." N.d. Www.youtube.com. Accessed June 7, 2023. https://youtu.be/N_ZHujsRoo0.

"Mark McCandlish." 2019. Pioneering Minds. October 22, 2019. https://www.pioneeringminds.com/mark-mccandlish/.

"Blueprint for a UFO (Presented by Dr. Steven Greer)." N.d. Www.youtube.com.. https://www.youtube.com/watch?v=ua0MMXJl3FM&list=PLAuYxV5og-5xIrkl_mRKfDcOa-SR7rBeu&index=3&t=38s.

The first public interview of Neil Armstrong, Buzz Aldrin, and Mike Collins after the first moon landing hints at this hidden reality. Their carefully chosen words, devoid of joy or patriotic exuberance, seem anomalous.

Bob Lazar provides valuable insights on antigravity technology. In a 1998 interview, he discussed the gravity wave generators and emitters in these crafts. They create an imbalance with Earth's gravity, causing repulsion and propulsion.

As per recent reports, our Tic Tac ships or ARVs, possibly manufactured at the Lockheed Skunkworks Plant 42 in California, utilize similar technology. Northup plant 29 is also rumored to be creating black project antigravity crafts.

The US Government's Perspective:
"A sparkling glare from Venus may induce mass hallucination."

The Skeptic's Corner:
Bob Lazar was late filing his tax return, hence his claims regarding UFOs can't be credible.

"Rare 1998 Investigation into Bob Lazar – Examine the Evidence Yourself!" n.d. Www.youtube.com. Accessed June 7, 2023. https://www.youtube.com/watch?v=JCXKiY0ovjM.

"Bob Lazar – Mind Bending Story That Is Real – Original 1989 Complete." N.d. Www.youtube.com. Accessed June 7, 2023. https://www.youtube.com/watch?v=A45mjzh8bfU.

"BREAKING NEWS: Dr. Greer Announces Discovery of 4 New Energy Technologies That Could Save the Earth!" n.d. Www.youtube.com. Accessed June 7, 2023. https://www.youtube.com/watch?v=0RnnH7vDbz4&t=102s.

QUESTION 2:

What kind of energy devices helped ETs get to earth and fly the universe?

Tucker's Perspective:

I am not sure, but they must be big ones. Grand Bob says we have all the power devices we need but the US Government patent office won't let them out.

The Fu Fu's Perspective:

Each type of alien craft has a different energy propulsion technology. We have been given technology from the EBENs, the Nordic races and the Tall Whites that include samples of element 115 which produces its own gravitational fields and antimatter energy. This internal gravitational field allows aliens or humans occupants to make immediate impossible stops, or 90 degree turns and speeds that reach 5,000 to 20,000 miles per hours which would turn humans into a mass of bloody hamburger.

Some ETs have developed nuclear powered craft with element 115 that produces its own gravitational field, there are other ET craft that fly with antimatter propulsion. Area 51 astrophysicist Bob Lazar was the first to tell the public that ARVs and ET Alien Crafts existed and about the propulsion drive element 115 in May of 1989. At the time, there were only 109 elements known on the periodic chart which cast a dispersion with scientists of the day (1989) only to be proven correct in 2013.

There are basic antigravity ARV ships that the US started testing in the mid 1950's that according to Capt. Bill Unhouse who testified on camera with DR Greer before he died that our ARVs function on six million of volts of electricity produced by some of the largest capacitors ever made in those days. The ARVs used two deep cell batteries to power the ARV for 30 minutes at a time for training purposes that were supposedly eventually replaced with US conventional nuclear reactors as the AREA 51 researchers could not perfect the element 115 propulsion drives. Several deaths at Area 51 have occurred working on reversing alien propulsion systems.

Both the Roswell crashes in 1947 and 1949 produced a small 12 by 12-inch square piece of what looked to be thick clear plexiglass material in the wreckage. After several years of research and testing it was determined these glass devices were power sources that would power any strength electrical device the scientists would plug into the alien plexiglass.

Los Alamos scientists determined this plexiglass could even power a small city and were probably a so-called zero-point energy device that could solve mankind's energy issues without pollution or the need for a power grid anymore. The alien plexiglass material appeared to pull energy from the air without any noticeable by-products of combustion or consumption.

Once of the military's diamond shaped reverse engineered nuclear reactor ARV/UFOs failed during a flight test. Betty Cash, Vickie Landrum and Vickie's grandson, Colby were in a traveling car (referred to as the Cash Landrum UFO accident) one night in Texas near Houston outskirts Dec 29. 1980. They saw a brilliant light and felt searing heat.

AI Generated art of Betty Cash incident

"Joe Rogan Experience #1315 – Bob Lazar & Jeremy Corbell." N.d. Www.youtube.com.https://youtube.com/watch?v=BEWz4SXfyCQ&t=1825s.

8 News NOW Las Vegas. 2019. "I-Team: A Look Back at 1989 Bob Lazar Interview; It Started New UFO Conversations." YouTube. https://www.youtube.com/watch?v=2GRjgBVw9Pk.

All of the victims received blistering radiation burns documented by the local hospital where they sought treatment for their injuries. The ladies filed a lawsuit against the military and were not successful in their effort but did eventually get the army to admit "a helicopter operation" did take place during a later chance conversation with a military helicopter pilot. Due to the military's historical direct interference and intimidation of physicians and with the investigation, no real proof could be established.

The key point to this question is the US government has access to this type of zero-point energy NOW. This gift of power proofing the entire world has occurred by direct transfer theft of ET and legitimate patented technology by US citizens to the US Government for the military to create a False Economic Vacuum. Patent holders who have come up with better clean energy patents have not been able to profit or share these technologies with the public which further cripples our economy.

The US Government securitized 6000 WORKING patents for propulsion, zero-point free energy devices, gravity control and weapons design including non-lethal weapons under the guise of national secrecy laws. This must stop now…Today and be released for every company to develop and compete to change our entire infrastructure to nonpolluting energy. That process would take 20 years. We would have to start now as we have run out of diesel in 5 years to transport our food to our tables.

Half of the world's population (3 billion) is too poor to have electricity to cook other than burning wood from trees. Burning wood deforests trees more than lumber companies do and is a bigger source of pollution or climate change than cars. If the 3 billion poor were to suddenly switch to the current gas/oil structure we have now by magic, the price of a gallon of gas suddenly would be over $1000 gallon that no one could afford. A free nonpolluting energy source could stop the world's pollution from cooking alone. As a result, we are still digging for oil and using inefficient solar and wind systems that need to be drastically replaced.

"Cash-Landrum UFO Incident – the Unexplained [Episode 4]." N.d. Www.youtube.com. https://www.youtube.com/watch?v=7V757DZ5Xwk.

"UFO Hunters: Life-Altering Alien Encounter (S2, E8) | Full Episode | History." https://www.youtube.com/watch?v=UPkW9XBX0fU.

The fact that the US government and private industries have colluded to stall and cloaked these free energies devices since Tesla inventions 100 years ago is unforgivable to contemplate in these modern times of need. Solar and wind don't even make a burp on the zeros point energy technology.

The US Government's Perspective:
Read My Lips, No New Taxes" (H. W. Bush)

The Skeptic's Corner:
There are no aliens so there are no abductions:

QUESTION 3:

Do we have interstellar spaceships that travel to the stars?

AI Generated art of alien spacecraft

Tucker's Perspective:
Yes.

"Homepage." 2023. Dr. Steven Greer. June 6, 2023. https://www.siriusdisclosure.com.

"BREAKING NEWS: Dr. Greer Announces Discovery of 4 New Energy Technologies That Could Save the Earth!" n.d. Www.youtube.com. https://www.youtube.com/watch?v=0RnnH7vDbz4&t=102s.

"Earthfiles – Reported and Edited by Linda Moulton Howe." N.d. Www.earthfiles.com. Accessed June 8, 2023. https://earthfiles.com.

The Fu Fu's Perspective:

Supposedly there are several interstellar spaceships. A few are named the USS Curtis Lemay, the USS Hoyt Vandenberg, and the USS Hellenkoetter which they also have terrestrial earth based naval war ships or locations and non-terrestrial interstellar ship names as reported by Gary McKinnon, the UK hacker who accessed NASA computer servers. Some of these ships are currently on 4.9 to 10.1 light year missions that will take less than 5 months to accomplish their respective routes using wormhole technology developed by the Nordics.

Tucker Carlson had a pathologist on his Fox Nation show named Gary Nolan, PhD a Sanford medical school professor who has have years of exposure to ET related issues. He was consulted by serious looking military officers on behalf of "military individuals, ground personnel and pilots exposed to UFO technology". In other words, the focus was for ARV UFO pilots and support personnel who fly the reverse Engineered f having neurological symptoms with abnormal MRI's showing "White Matter Disease" when they had prolonged exposure to Antigravity Craft. Dr. Nolan has been on several other video programs regarding UFOs.

The US Government's Perspective:

President Trump said, "there may be UFOs, but I don't particularly believe in it."

The Skeptic's Corner:

If NASA says there are no aliens. There are no galactic spaceships. But now we need to get the UFO nuts to shut up.

QUESTION 4:
How do the various ETs races control their anti-gravity, electromagnetic, nuclear powered or antimatter crafts?

Tucker's Perspective:

With their hands.

Fridman, Lex. 2022. "Garry Nolan: UFOs and Aliens | Lex Fridman Podcast #262." YouTube. https://www.youtube.com/watch?v=uTCc2-1tbBQ.

"NASA Panel Studying UFO Sightings Says Stigma and Poor Data Pose Challenges." 2023. NBC News. May 31, 2023. https://www.nbcnews.com/science/ufos-and-aerial-phenomena/nasa-ufo-unidentified-aerial-phenomena-panel-hearing-rcna87034.

The Fu Fu's Perspective:

ETs have flat hand consoles like flat desks with TV monitors where they place their elongated fingers in ergonomic hand depressions to control the craft. Other ET advanced races control their craft with their consciousness, telepathy, and neural linking such as what Elon Musk is just developing. (Richard Doty GAIA TV Interviews) Mark McCandlish discussed alien hand control ball control on our first ARV with a suspended ball held by a curved T mount like a mouse on a computer.

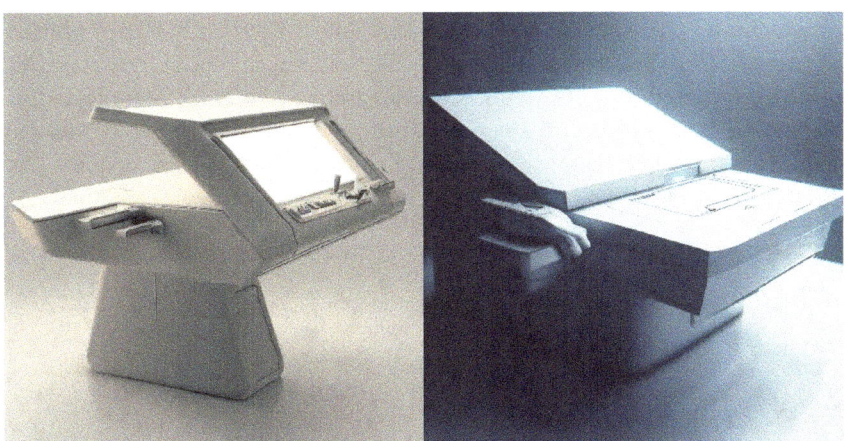

AI Generated art of alien control panels

The US Government's Perspective:

We do not have antigravity technology (2022 UFO congressional hearings)

The Skeptic's Corner:

Aliens can't steer with their fingers without causing crashes. You need two hands on the wheel to drive as everyone knows.

QUESTION 5:
How long does a radio signal take to go 39.1 lights years to the EBEN Planet Serpo in the Zeta Reticuli system?

Tucker's Perspective:

A long time but Grand Bob Says the aliens figured out a way to do it in a few months.

The Fu Fu's Perspective:

The travel distances are much shorter than previously thought with worm holes, black holes and stargate portals.

Motorola was contracted to produce a burst communication system that can send a signal in 5 hours to Zeta Reticuli, 39.1 light years away from earth. This is a thousand times faster than the speed of light. New research with instant particle entanglement associated with quantum physics is just being developed.

The military discovered this technology back in 1949 when they housed one of the EBEN survivors from the Roswell Crash at Los Alamos who shared this new physics with the researchers who help design this communication equipment. Even Harvard professors and other Ivy league professors nowadays are not taught the new physics that makes this technology possible.

AI Generated art of Rulers timeline and signal getting there over long distances.

Students and other researchers at SETI are left still thinking basic radio waves are going to reach out over millions of light years to reach an inhabited planet and wait another million years for a reply. It is shameful the public has been kept in the dark for so long. Just Plain Shameful.

The US Government's Perspective:

There have never been any communications from SETI or NASA with aliens.

The Skeptic's Corner:

SETI says there are no signals they have heard from space and anyone who says different needs to be examined.

QUESTION 6:

What do you do if you see a spacecraft land or crash?

Tucker's Perspective:

Don't approach or get underneath to avoid potential radiation exposure and immediately notify your parents or teacher if you see it at school.

The Fu Fu's Perspective:

First be aware if a craft is hovering over you get to the side of the craft as soon as possible at least 200 feet away or take shelter in a house or car to protect from either direct radiation or extremely powerful electromagnetic waves. Notify authorities of any landing immediately so if this is an abduction event someone knows of it immediately. ET craft have the ability to shine energy systems to surrounding witnesses that cause hypnotic, amnesia or paralytic effects. Also, remember, Dr Gary Nolan warning about those military personnel who have worked around UFOs for extended times can come down with "white matter disease" or brain damage visualized on MRIs (Fox Nation Streaming with Tucker Carlson)

If the UFO has crashed or does crash and ET bodies are visible remember some species of aliens like insectoids do emit a toxic formulation of their internal organs and may also have protective devices on them that activate when approached by individuals who want to render aid. In many cases, there have been instances where the UFO craft themselves are toxic and have inured and killed retrieval teams. (Richard Doty, Gaia.com would be the best source of information on alien craft retrieval hazards)

"Ariel School UFO Incident." 2022. Wikipedia. October 31, 2022. https://en.wikipedia.org/wiki/Ariel_School_UFO_incident.

7NEWS Australia. 2021. "Westall's 50-Year-Old UFO Sighting Emerges Again | 7NEWS." YouTube. https://www.youtube.com/watch?v=yePuBSftyhQ.

EBENs, Greys, Tall Whites and Nordics are more closely related to humans and are not considered toxic but have a different vascular system. EBENs have a heart and lung functioning as a single unit and they do seek help if injured. IVs can be started but should have a slow IV drip rate with an isotonic solution depending on the species of aliens (however NACL solutions could be toxic in some species of aliens), arms and legs can be splinted. Dr. Kit Green MD (a CIA consultant) and Dr. Greer might be the best sources for stabilizing ETs.

Reptilian (Quantaloid) or Trantaloid (Insectoid) species are more problematic in approaching. Trantaloids have more of a history of lethal danger for military ground retrieval teams to approach without wearing hazmat suits with self-contained breathing apparatus.

AI Generated art of crashed alien spacecraft

The US Government's Perspective:

There is no need to fear any boogeymen harming you if your taxes are paid up. Biden said, "he was arrested during a civil right march."

The Skeptic's Corner:

There is a greater chance of being struck by lightning than seeing a UFO.

QUESTION 7:

Have we ever been to the Moon or Mars with antigravity technology other than NASA control rocket technology?

Tucker's Perspective:

Yes, with our UFOs called ARVs.

The Fu Fu's Perspective:

Yes, we have taken missions and voyages to the moon, the planet Mars and several moons of Saturn and Jupiter with our ARVs. We have had mini-bases on the moon, Mars and other planets and aliens have bases on the earth, the moon and other planets. We have been given technology from several species of aliens for over 70 decades and we have been off planet with antigravity technology for that same timeline.

1AI Generated art of UFOs in formation flying in orbit around the Moon.

One of the NASA contractors, Donna Hare said she was hired to work on space photographs and was privy to see technicians that "airbrush" the

UFOs and ETs out of NASA public pictures of the moon and space to avoid the public from seeing proof of UFOs on ETs. Other technicians were ordered to burn pictures of UFO pictures that were too populated with UFOs to be airbrushed and were threatened if they looked at the pictures before burning the NASA pictures.

Most ET researchers and UFO quoted astrophysicists feel the moon is hollow, was towed into position 50,000 years ago, it is too round and perfectly positioned to be natural, is a reconnaissance base for several species of ETs to monitor the earth and other planets in our solar system.

The current ongoing race of our private billionaire rocketeers like Elon Musk, Branson (who is out of the space race for now) and Jeff Bezos are actually and secretly competing in a deadly serious dash for the military's eventual release of antigravity technology to whoever come out on top financially for our government. Right now, rocket technology contracts are the only technology contracts these billionaires can play with and are allowed to bid for NASA money. May the best billionaire win.

The military must fund this critical clandestine race to deflect the anger that will surface when disclosure takes place. The military must cage this secret release of anti-gravity technology to a private corporation who will appear to be responsible for its invention. Colonel Philips Corso proved this in his book, The Day after Roswell, with the secret release of alien laser technology, computer chips and fiber optic technology to various private military subcontractors in the 50s and 60s.

This winning rocket corporation must prove it can work the military so both will profit, and the public anger will eventually subside and be forgotten when you can drive to work in your George Jetson car. Not an electric or gas driven one by the way.

The US Government's Perspective:
There are no such things as aliens in our bedrooms or on the moon.

The Skeptic's Corner:
There is no proof the moon is hollow or that Darth Vader lives there.

"The NASA Conspiracy: Donna Hare Witness Testimony (Airbrushed Moon Photos?)." n.d. Www.youtube.com. Accessed June 8, 2023. https://www.youtube.com/watch?v=tEBLmWhx1K0.

QUESTION 8:
Did our astronauts who went to the moon see aliens or find out if the moon is hollow?

Tucker's Perspective:
Yes, I watched a show that said we did see aliens on the moon from our astronauts.

The Fu Fu's Perspective:
Yes, not only did we see aliens and recorded radio communications about seeing aliens between the Johnson Space Center in Houston and the Apollo Lunar Lander, but the Astronauts were told by the greys who have bases on the moon and Mars not to come back to the moon. That is the biggest reason we have not been back and not from the lack of money or support as NSAA claimed.

The initial Apollo mission was partially designed to recover proof of life and occupation by alien races which all the astronauts in all subsequent Apollo missions witnessed. When Neil Armstrong landed on the moon, they saw 6 interstellar star ships that lined the perimeter of a crater watching Neil Armstrong jumping off the lunar lander's stairs taking the first step on the moon.

There were so many daily sightings by each Apollo mission that they referred to the aliens as, "seeing Santa Claus' each time the astronauts saw an ET or UFO. These secret radio communication recordings were captured by HAM radio operators on open and closed channels.

The US Government's Perspective:
Masks are not needed for COVID outbreaks (CDC and WHO) because we don't have enough.

HISTORY. 2021. "The UnXplained: Apollo 12 Uncovers a Hollow Moon (Season 2) | History." YouTube. https://www.youtube.com/watch?v=U6bQh1EU5n0.

"The Hollow Moon Theory; Is the Moon an Artificial Satellite?" n.d. Gaia. https://www.gaia.com/article/the-hollow-moon-theory-is-the-moon-an-artificial-satellite.

"How Masks Went from Don't-Wear to Must-Have during the Coronavirus Pandemic." n.d. Wired. https://www.wired.com/story/how-masks-went-from-dont-wear-to-must-have/.

The Skeptic's Corner:
The moon is not hollow and did not ring like a bell when the lunar orbiter crashed.

QUESTION 9:
Why has the Government not come forward with all the ET information and Technology that they have been compiling for almost 100 years and denied ANY contact with captured craft, ETs or wreckage?

Tucker's Perspective:
Grand Bob Says that governments don't always tell the truth and that I should.

_____

"Hollow Moon." 2023. Wikipedia. June 5, 2023. https://en.wikipedia.org/wiki/Hollow_Moon#:~:text=The%20Moon%20rang%20like%20a%20bell.

The Fu Fu's Perspective:

Apparently, our government's secret battles with all nations and races of ETs are more important than the human element of representative truth the government is supposed to prioritize and dignify have failed. Therefore, so parts of our government do what they do best and simply LIE.

Presidents have lied, disinformed and misrepresented the truth, legislators from both legislative branches have lied, and our justice department have misrepresented the truth. The military intelligence divisions spend lifetimes and decades of manipulation the public through the expert use of disinformation supported by the need for national security originally put into action by President Truman.

Trillions and trillions of dollars have mysteriously drained into secret antigravity, zero-point energy technology development and off-planet non-rocket propulsion technology by hundreds of black project diversions of taxpayer's money with nothing available for the civilian sector yet. The government has trillions of reasons to lie about ET technology and protect this path of money flow with every means possible.

According to several sources from GAIA.com, Earthfiles.com, and SiriusDsiclosure.com, Eisenhower met with aliens at several AF bases and had conversations with aliens that resulted in treaties being signed allowing the aliens access to resources here on earth.

Carlson, Peter. 2004. "Ike and the Alien Ambassadors." Washington Post, February 19, 2004. https://www.washingtonpost.com/archive/lifestyle/2004/02/19/ike-and-the-alien-ambassadors/4698c544-1dc8-4573-8b8d-2b48d2a6305c/.

"Did President Eisenhower Meet Aliens at Air Force Bases?" n.d. Gaia. Accessed June 8, 2023. https://www.gaia.com/article/eisenhower-meets-aliens-holloman-afb.

"UFOs and FLYING SAUCERS." n.d. Accessed June 8, 2023. https://www.eisenhowerlibrary.gov/sites/default/files/2020-11/UFOs%20and%20Flying%20Saucers.pdf.

President Nixon supposedly left his secret service detail in Miami, Florida and commandeered a presidential limo and drove secretly by himself to Jackie Gleason's house. Gleason was a good friend and golfing buddy of Nixon and took him to Homestead AFB nearby, met William Rumsfeld at the base gate and let Jackie Gleason see a deceased alien in frozen cryogenic enclosures.

Jackie Gleason was an avid UFO enthusiast with a house shaped like a UFO. He was stunned that he got to see an alien and told his wife, and immediately afterwards, several tabloid newspapers ran with the story. Both President Reagan a significant UFO enthusiast and President Jimmy Carter also related seeing a UFO and reporting them. President Reagan was highly briefed on the ET CIA briefing including the 1965-1978 exchange program with EBENs from the planet Serpo.

Reagan privately asked Russian President Mickell Gorbachev at a UN meeting if UFOs or Aliens invade America would he assist the US in fighting aliens together and Gorbachev relied, "Yes".

Truman was briefed on UFOs and was fearful of Americans finding out ETs were real. President Truman originally created and authorized the CIA to help hide ET/UFO information from the public. President Kennedy created and authorized NASA to compete with the Military SPACE RACE and created the Defense Intelligence Agency (DIA) for gathering similar intelligence that the CIA would not share with his office.

"The Night JACKIE GLEASON Completely Lost It - UFO SHOCKER!" n.d. Www.youtube.com. Accessed June 8, 2023. https://www.youtube.com/watch?v=Voi20F8Gz70.

"Regan 27A Classified Alien Briefing." n.d. Www.youtube.com. Accessed June 8, 2023. https://www.youtube.com/watch?v=yl36NJJ0Pf8.

Marik von Rennenkampff, Opinion Contributor. 2021. "Biden Should Channel Reagan, Ask Putin about UFOs at Summit." The Hill. June 15, 2021. https://thehill.com/opinion/international/558305-biden-should-channel-reagan-ask-putin-about-ufos-at-summit/.

"UFOS: The Evidence No One Is Talking About." n.d. Gaia. Accessed June 8, 2023. https://www.gaia.com/article/ufos-the-evidence-no-one-is-talking-about.

An exceptional article regarding Truman and a much larger number of UFOs and ET bodies were recovered in the US according to William Cooper who supposedly had some very deep information as a navy veteran. He has been listed as critical conspiracy theories by every breathing skeptic. According to Cooper, between January 1947 and December 1952 at least 16 crashed or downed alien craft, 65 alien bodies, and 1 live alien were recovered between the US, Norway, and Mexico.

William Cooper died in a gunfight with deputies who Cooper also injured by gunfire. Cooper was being arrested for potential IRS fraud. IRS charges are also a potential known tool to punish or force compliance with governmental secrecy intentions or certain political or last-ditch ways to silence opposition. People on both sides of the fence find his behavior concerning but Cooper's ET information does seem to be supported by some in the UFO community. Segments of this article are supported by similar factual stories by Linda Moulton Howe and Dr. Greer. I find this article stunning as it addresses many incidents not normally discussed.

If you need any more recent reminders of how the IRS is weaponized to bully whistleblowers just ask the reporter that exposed Twitter closeted info on Hunter Biden and how the FBI helped throw the 2020 election.

As Part of Truman's UFO legacy, Truman supposedly started the Majestic Twelve or MJ-12. MJ-12 top secret documents were reportedly given to UFO journalist Linda Moulton Howe by photographic film. The film was developed to reveal that 12 top ranking military and governmental scientific leaders were picked by Truman to secretly contain, professionally disinform the public and secretly benefit by advanced alien propulsion/energy systems by obtained UFO technology gathered by the retrieval of alien craft and extraterrestrial entities accompanying these crafts. The FBI on their website debunks the information and the UFO community says this is proof of the MJ-12.

"Majestic 12 and the Secret Government." n.d. Www.cs.mcgill.ca. https://www.cs.mcgill.ca/~abatko/interests/conspiracy/mj12/.

Archive, View Author, and Get author RSS feed. 2023. "IRS Opened Probe into Matt Taibbi's Taxes after Twitter Dump." May 24, 2023. https://nypost.com/2023/05/24/irs-opened-probe-into-matt-taibbis-taxes-after-twitter-dump/.

"Ancient Aliens: Top Secret Documents for Majic Eyes Only (Season 12, Episode 9) | History." n.d. Www.youtube.com. Accessed June 8, 2023. https://www.youtube.com/watch?v=Zq0Ae3eO5Lw.

President Kennedy supposedly shared the UFO/ET information with his brother and their mistress Marilyn Monroe. After both Kennedy brothers' trysts with Marilyn Monroe, they both became fearful of continuing a relationship and stopped communicating with her. She became angry and wrote a letter announcing she would go public with her information on UFOs.

Monroe reportedly committed suicide under suspicious circumstances. President Kenney also supposedly told the Joint Chiefs that he was going to go public with the covert UFO related information ten days prior to his assassination. As you may, the skeptics say this information is debunked and the UFO researchers say this is proof of Kennedys death.

Estimating that our government is honest less than 50% of the time from political assertions who would you believe, a 30-year veteran of the air force willing to share copies of official documentation of UFOs or a sitting president denouncing UFOs?

The Brooking Institute was also contracted to generate an opinion of whether to release the lid on ET and UFO information. Here is their response, "Public realization that intelligent beings live on other planets could bring about profound changes, or even the collapse of our civilizations, Societies sure of their own place have disintegrated when confronted by a superior society". 1960 Brookings institute research paper contracted by NASA.

"Linda Moulton Howe / Extraterrestrial Technology." n.d. Dwij.org. https://dwij.org/pathfinders/linda_moulton_howe/linda_m_h12.htm.

"Mystery Wire – How Marilyn Monroe's Death May Be Linked to UFO's." 2021. WOWK 13 News. May 27, 2021. https://www.wowktv.com/news/u-s-world/mystery-wire-how-marilyn-monroes-death-may-be-linked-to-ufos/.

Ross, Alex. 2019. "UFO Festival Speaker Alleges Marilyn Monroe's Death Was Alien Cover-Up." Roswell Daily Record. July 6, 2019. https://www.rdrnews.com/news/local/ufo-festival-speaker-alleges-marilyn-monroe-s-death-was-alien-cover-up/article_60674ebf-0fae-5bb8-a9ba-abb13e4c1448.html.

HISTORY. 2018. "Ancient Aliens: Was JFK Silenced? (Season 12, Episode 9) | History." YouTube. https://www.youtube.com/watch?v=a_AW3bUxumI.

Blake, John. 2013. "Of Course Presidents Lie | CNN Politics." CNN. November 24, 2013. https://www.cnn.com/2013/11/24/politics/presidents-lie.

The US Government's Perspective:

I have previously stated, and I repeat now, that the United States plans no military intervention in Cuba," – John F. Kennedy.

The Skeptic's Corner:

Uncle Sam would never get in bed with Aliens so just forget about aliens.

QUESTION 10:

Is the technology that ETs offer or the attraction that we can become a member of the galactic brotherhood of the Galactic Empire like dealing with a fox in the henhouse. Are we powerful enough to remain human or become slaves of the advanced races?

Tucker's Perspective:

I am not sure.

The Fu Fu's Perspective:

That depends on your perspective of life, perspective of religion, your upbringings, and your desire to remain either an independent thinker or a cog in a wheel you have no control over in a society that forces your participation or acknowledges and accepts your individuality. Proof for both levels of fear and trust have been demonstrated in conflicts with alien races. Some species have fought battles with other races of aliens to protect humans and protect the earth.

Some UFOs controlled by ETs have shut down the US nuclear missile silos batteries near Malmstrom AFB in Montana, to demonstrate their willingness to protect humanity and earth from extinction. In some cases, aliens have activated the go codes for Russian nuclear missiles to launch to the point that the Russian generals were so fearful the missiles would fire on the US and start a total nuclear war.

The aliens stepped in at the last minute and deactivated the launch sequence before total nuclear commitment was reached. Again, this was a display of alien technology that demonstrated the power that these ET races have over all human militaries around the world.

"Ex-Air Force Personnel: UFOs Deactivated Nukes." n.d. Www.cbsnews.com. https://www.cbsnews.com/news/ex-air-force-personnel-ufos-deactivated-nukes/.

Quest TV. 2022. "'It Was Definitely a UFO That Shut down Our Missiles' Aliens Stop Nukes? | the Unexplained Files." YouTube. https://www.youtube.com/watch?v=vwzBO3L5GSQ.

In several meetings with President Eisenhower to sign a 1954 alien-human treaty with the US regarding abductions and nuclear testing. Eisenhower has several meetings with Val "Valiant" Thor a Nordic ET and other interviews with EBENS, the species of aliens who crashed and were hosted here on earth. The ETs said to Eisenhower, "that all the nuclear testing by Russia and the US were tearing the fabric of interdimensional space boundaries throughout the universe when air burst nuclear detonations occurred".

Reportedly, the aliens were going to stop further nuclear testing by any means possible. Nuclear testing moved underground until all nuclear weapon nations testing was agreed to stop. However, humans continued to violate the treaty for several decades. North Korea may be the new target of the aliens and may have stopped their nuclear program with an underground nuclear blast destroying the mountain in May of 2918 and perhaps temporarily slowing the North Korean's ability to manufacture their nuclear missiles. However, recently they have been back to testing missiles again so that makes that story less likely.

The US Government's Perspective:
Electric Cars are much better for the environment, and they won't make us dependent on China and Russia for resources...

The Skeptic's Corner:
Electric Cars are not Aliens Cars.

"'Aliens Have Made Treaties with the US Government' | UFO Witness." n.d. Www.youtube.com. https://www.youtube.com/watch?v=-FHaGFkHULo.

Noble, Barnes &. n.d. "We Will Never Let You Down: Encounters with Val Thor and Journeys beyond Earth|Paperback." Barnes & Noble. Accessed June 8, 2023. https://www.barnesandnoble.com/w/we-will-never-let-you-down-elena-danaan/1140545030?ean=9798765513620.

"Exclusive: Nuke Test Mountain Collapse May Be Why Kim Jong-Un Actually Shut down Site." 2018. South China Morning Post. April 25, 2018. https://www.scmp.com/news/china/diplomacy-defence/article/2143171/north-koreas-nuclear-test-site-has-collapsed-and-may-be-why-kim-jong-un.

S, Robert, ers, Media relations| May 10, 2018May 15, and 2018. 2018. "Radar Reveals Details of Mountain Collapse after North Korea's Most Recent Nuclear Test." Berkeley News. May 10, 2018. https://news.berkeley.edu/2018/05/10/radar-reveals-details-of-mountain-collapse-after-north-koreas-most-recent-nuclear-test/.

QUESTION 11:

Should we only allow our governmental military to benefit from this technology or should the advanced antigravity craft and advanced energy sources be shared with the public to benefit?

Tucker's Perspective:

I want to have this technology to travel like the Jetsons.

The Fu Fu's Perspective:

Everyone should know the history of human interaction with aliens and the fact aliens predated humans on this planet for hundreds of millions of years and during that time we have had millions of contacts with many species of aliens. Aliens really do travel like George Jetson with their families and for the sake of exploration, research, and experimentation.

AI Generated Art of A person riding a dinosaur with a group of UFOs flying over it.

The US Government's Perspective:

George Washington's teeth were not made from wood, rather they were a combination of gold, ivory, lead, and human and animal teeth. And the cherry tree chopping tale never happened at all. We Have been telling these falsehoods for 200 years.

The Skeptic's Corner:

I don't believe in aliens but just in case let me know if any alien technology comes up on Kickstarter.

QUESTION 12:

I haven't seen any aliens or UFO's, why should I believe anyone that

these entities exist?

Tucker's Perspective:
I believe Grand Bob believes in them and I believe what I saw in Sedona.

The Fu Fu's Perspective:
The truth is there have been millions of people who have had direct contact with aliens, hundreds of thousands of pictures, videos, and confirmed by seeing off world wreckage. This wreckage has been captured since 1947 and if you don't believe in the fact ETs are here, you are ignoring highly professional, credible people who have multiple experiences and careers dealing with these ET contacts.

UFOs have even appeared over the White House on several occasions over several weekends in 1952 with the air force being scrambled and visualizing the UFOs with actual radar tracking speeds of beyond any man-made craft for that time period. Science has confirmed the life has existed in outer space on the space station and on other planets. The days of discrediting the sighting of UFOs and destroying the lives of honest citizens of the world who have been proven beyond a shadow of a doubt with hard proof of alien human contact.

Mathematically, it would be highly irresponsible to ignore the reality that other life exists beyond earth, but the fact has been proven beyond a shadow of a doubt with actual live beings. Trillions of solar systems exist in our galaxy and there are trillions of galaxies therefore… there is almost an unlimited number of planets that have life.

Belief in the Bible is based on faith and the positive experience of what letting God and Jesus into your life is proven, I submit also that there are volumes of ET proof in human literature, newspaper articles, media, and books. I have faith that the majority of experiencers, the government and civilian witnesses are also truthful. Certain editions of the Bible confirm the presence of what could be interpreted as UFO and ET entities as descriptions of angles in some testimonies, ETs appear identical as angelic in form and substance. Many modern-day astronauts have confirmed angelic ETs in space and on the moon.

The US Government's Perspective:
Henry Ford was the first person to invent the car, not Karl Benz…

The Skeptic's Corner:
I don't believe in religion or aliens, but just in case I get abducted I will buy that necklace with a cross from you to wear.

QUESTION 13:
Can UFOs go underwater or pass-through rock or dirt.

Tucker's Perspective:
Yes, Grand Bob let me watch a TV show that showed a real UFO coming in and out of the water.

The Fu Fu's Perspective:
Yes, many UFOs over many decades have been filmed by military and civilian personnel diving into water and clocked over several hundred miles an hour through water by ship and submarine sonar. Other UFOs have been seen disappearing into granite mountains and other rock formations. A large amount of UFO activity has been seen around volcanoes with UFO circling and diving directly into them. UFOs and ETs have been confirmed by "experts" as having possible trans-dimensional abilities to have their atoms pass through the atoms of other materials at will.

"Bible Verses about Aliens." n.d. Biblestudytools.com. https://www.biblestudytools.com/topical-verses/bible-verses-about-aliens/.
There are multiple videos showing UFOs going in and out of water from military naval ships.

AI Generated Art of an Alien ship coming out of the water.

Homeland Security aircraft in Puerto Rico where in this video the UFO splits into two UFOs and enter the water while traveling just under 100 mph and enters water and exits with no loss of speed.

---

published, Mindy Weisberger. 2021. "Spherical UFO Plunges into the Ocean in US Navy Footage." Livescience.com. May 25, 2021. https://www.livescience.com/ufo-flies-and-dives-navy-footage.html.

"Video Shows Spherical UFO off California Disappearing into Ocean." 2021. FOX 10 Phoenix. May 18, 2021. https://www.fox10phoenix.com/news/video-shows-spherical-ufo-off-california-disappearing-into-ocean.

"What Flies in the in the Air, Zips through the Ocean, and Splits in Two? Scientifically Investigating the Aguadilla UFO Incident." 2021. WWLP. February 12, 2021. https://www.wwlp.com/news/what-flies-in-the-in-the-air-zips-through-the-ocean-and-splits-in-two-scientifically-investigating-the-aguadilla-ufo-incident/.

A larger triangle UFO the size of a destroyer battleship has been seen and supposedly filmed rising out of the water by navy personnel during "lights out" exercises. The largest UFO ever seen was observed by two Chilean Air Force pilots was the length of 10 aircraft carriers near the coastline of Antofagasta, Chile , South America. Aircraft carriers are over 1000 feet long which makes this UFO nearly 2 miles long.

Naval ships and submarines have clocked USOs or Underwater Submerged Objects at speed of 500 knots which is an unheard-of speed since the fastest nuclear subs can only travel underwater up to 60 knots or Russians supposedly have super cavitation torpedoes that create an air bubble around them that may go up to 200 knots. For context, consider that the black marlin, the fastest fish in the world, can reach speeds of 80 mph or approximately 69.5 knots.

One of the most proof positive and documented UFOs sightings in history was the size of 7 jumbo jets was seen circling a Japan Airlines jumbo jet captain flying to Alaska. The entire encounter was recorded by ATC voice and FAA radar data. The CIA in a secret briefing meeting with FAA staff confiscated the FAA radar data tapes and voice recording but a copy was made by the regional director of the FAA crash investigations team, John Callahan.

The FAA tape was played during a US national press conference organized by Dr. Greer in 2001. (See the following video of that conference arranged by Dr Greer with 20 other highly respectable and credible witness testimonies that was stopped from national broadcasting by all US national media stations per agreements with US intelligence agencies. However, it was broadcast internationally to all other countries.

"Underwater Speed Record." 2021. Wikipedia. November 20, 2021. https://en.wikipedia.org/wiki/Underwater_speed_record.

"2001 National Press Club Event (Presented by Dr. Steven Greer)." n.d. Www.youtube.com. https://www.youtube.com/watch?v=4DrcG7VGgQU.

"UFO Buzzes Japan Airlines - (FAA's Callahan Reveals)." n.d. Www.youtube.com. Accessed June 8, 2023. https://youtu.be/V4WTid3O0VE.

"2001 National Press Club Event (Presented by Dr. Steven Greer)." n.d. Www.youtube.com. https://www.youtube.com/watch?v=4DrcG7VGgQU.

The US Government's Perspective:

Thomas Edison did not invent the light bulb. He borrowed/stole it from other inventors.

The Skeptic's Corner:

I know my car won't go through water so neither will a UFO.

QUESTION 14:

Can UFOs become invisible?

Tucker's Perspective:

Yes, UFOs and some ETs can disappear in a second. Aliens will trade things.

The Fu Fu's Perspective:

Yes, the ETs and their craft can cloak themselves. The alien craft can travel in different dimensions, travel through portals, wormholes and they can disappear with refraction and diffraction of light waves. The technology is like bending light waves using optics like Lindell lens and/or camouflaged digital sensors that can currently mimic the background on military vehicles.

AI Generated Art of a UFO disappearing in the sky.

The trans dimensional abilities of ETs and UFOs to pass from one dimension to another also make them invisible to those in another dimension. The military now has holographic projection technology to make enemy pilots see a squadron of "projected" US fighters bearing down on them. Phasing in and out or shifting light perception is the result.

The fact these ETs can be trans dimensional and have portal egress that explains so many other sightings, pictures and missing individuals or other beings/creatures. This use of portals is historically timeless and can include visualizations of extinct animals such as dinosaurs like plesiosaurs which explains the Loch Ness Monster, Champ and other "tentacled sea monsters', flying dinosaurs like modern day pterodactyls, age old Sasquatches or Big Foot sightings or, Red Eyed Moth men who appears or come in and out of dimensional time zones.

Also, people who disappear right in front of other witnesses and numerous other incredible sightings from credible people of all these strange phenomena we once thought were hoaxes or tall tales. You have to go back to the dawn of human existence and recalculate the lack of explanations for these sights of strange animals and apply new facts to these strangest sightings are part of human history. There were two CIA operatives who witnessed two other agents disappear in front of their eyes in the 60's.

The US Government's Perspective:
War of the Worlds by Orson Welles 1938 public radio program did not cause panic as only a few households were surveyed even listening to it. So how did the story of the "panic" grow over the years? Slate blames newspapers, which allegedly "seized the opportunity presented by Welles' program to discredit radio as a source of news. The newspaper industry sensationalized the panic to prove to advertisers, and regulators, that radio management was irresponsible and not to be trusted.

The Skeptic's Corner:
Invisible aliens are like having invisible money, both are not real.

QUESTION 15:
Is there proof that UFOs were seen before 1947?

Tucker's Perspective:
Tucker: I wasn't born yet, ask Grand Bob.

The Fu Fu's Perspective:
UFOs were constantly seen and photographed during WWII and took the shape of red, white, or orange plasma balls of light. These UFOs were even called Foo Fighters trailing in large numbers near the wings and fuselage of our fighter and bombers for years. UFOs were heavily seen during the

development of the atomic bomb development.

Throughout recorded history, all civilizations and religions have referenced star beings and UFOs in various mediums, from cave drawings to literature. However, widely respected publications, such as the Smithsonian and Time Magazine, often avoid confronting these facts directly. They instead present them in ways that align with contemporary scientific consensus and political correctness.

AI Generated Art of a UFO in the sky

The US Government's Perspective:

"Extraterrestrial life has never been discovered, but that doesn't mean it doesn't exist" (NASA, astrobiologist Lindsay Hays) 99% of NASA has not been briefed or allowed to know about the ET or UFO phenomenon.

The Skeptic's Corner:

Don't count your UFOs before they crash.

QUESTION 16:
Have humans learned to time travel or change human events with ET technology.

Tucker's Perspective:

Yes, I saw it on Ancient Aliens.

Pooley, Jefferson, and Michael J Socolow. 2013. "Orson Welles' War of the Worlds Did Not Touch off a Nationwide Hysteria. Few Americans Listened. Even Fewer Panicked." Slate Magazine. Slate. October 29, 2013. https://slate.com/culture/2013/10/orson-welles-war-of-the-worlds-panic-myth-the-infamous-radio-broadcast-did-not-cause-a-nationwide-hysteria.html.

The Fu Fu's Perspective:

Yes, time portals and star gates have been created and discovered but these technologies are highly guarded and protected to avoid changing human history. Small changes have occurred by accident and by intention, but the US military has been studying and participating in time travel since 1960.

Some report that General George Washington before a battle encountered an angelic ET or child from the future that encouraged the attack across the Potomac River.

Portals have been opened using high energy lasers and other direct energy weapons and varying small micro nuclear explosions. There has even been blowback products and items and even bodies that have been thrown out of the portal into our dimension from opening these portals. Some suggest that one reason the Iraq war was fought beyond the public cover of finding weapons of mass destruction (WMD) was to secure a known time travel portals or stargates in Iraq.

The US Government's Perspective:

On Man.... Alcohol is better than Gas. You can drink it or burn it and you can even make it at home. It is a great portal for stargazing while I hug you. (Joe Biden or his Look-A-Like) If you keep telling the same lie long enough more people will believe you and you can win them over.

The Skeptic's Corner:

Is 15 percent ethanol safe for your car? The EPA is issuing an emergency waiver to allow widespread sale of 15% ethanol blend that is usually prohibited between June 1 and Sept. 15 due to smog concerns.

"The History of Foo Fighters (No, Not Those Ones)." n.d. Blaze TV. https://www.blaze.tv/series/ancient-aliens/history-foo-fighters-no-not-those-ones.

Wikipedia Contributors. 2019. "Foo Fighter." Wikipedia. Wikimedia Foundation. November 20, 2019. https://en.wikipedia.org/wiki/Foo_fighter.

AI Generated Art of a Star Gate Portal

QUESTION 17:

<u>Why do we still have organization like SETI and NASA that depend on caveman technology to communicate with other worlds or get around with rocket technology that can barely escape earth's gravity without the expenditure of 90% of its fuel to get 200 miles into space?</u>

Tucker's Perspective:
Tucker: I will have to ask Grand Bob.

The Fu Fu's Perspective:
Both agencies are now nothing more but probably diversions and subtle disinformation nowadays. SETI is supposedly privately funded but gets grants from the US government and other money from the feds get there in various ways.

The WOW! The signal was first observed on August 15, 1977, by the Ohio State University's Big Ear radio telescope near the 21-cm hydrogen line at 1420 MHz and has not been redetected.

SETI listens and does not transmit. Also, it was determined that the frequencies to transmit are based on an inverse square law of physics and to get a signal out to the far reaches of a star system that we have confirmed as the Goldilocks exoplanet region that has probable life would require far more power than what is currently used to transmit any significant distance by conventional means.

SETI never communicated with other worlds officially on their own or if they did, they never shared it with the public tax money that helped partially fund them. One of the directors of SETI was a huge naysayer of UFOs who has now has now changed his tune. However, Motorola did obtain the technology by captured EBENs and did transmit to the EBENs home planet, to Zeta Reticuli in 1952. So really SETI is essentially useless and is another prop being used by the government for hiding the truth.

But none of that SETI history really matters anyway because officially, Earth already made communication with ETs when the ETS came here millions of years ago. The movie, Contact was another wannabe Hollywood experiment of how the public would respond to the possibility of a contact and the issues surrounding the possible religious impact of ET contact.

NASA had two sides to it. The civilian component and the Secret Military/governmental intelligence component. NASA is almost out of the space business as private corporations have done better jobs launching high tech rockets into space to compete better than as most of these private industries have been deprived of the Militaries antigravity technology.

Staff and AP • •. n.d. "Will High-Ethanol Gasoline Ruin Your Car Engine? What to Know about E15." NBC 5 Dallas-Fort Worth. https://www.nbcdfw.com/news/national-international/what-is-ethanol-and-is-e15-safe-to-use-in-your-car-what-you-need-to-know/2938500/.

"SETI Wants Your Money to Look at Nothing – CEH." n.d. Crev.info. Accessed June 8, 2023. https://crev.info/2020/02/seti-wants-your-money-to-look-at-nothing/.

May 2018, Jeanna Bryner 10. n.d. "Congress Wants to Spend $10 Million to Search for Aliens, and Texas Is to Thank." Livescience.com. https://www.livescience.com/62529-congress-search-for-intelligent-aliens.html.

Elon Musk, Jeff Bezos, Bob Bigelow and Branson know or certainly should know that the military perfected antigravity (AG) technology in 1954 and these billionaires are jockeying for the big Anti-Gravity (AG) contracts ultimately. The covert military government is making these billionaires play blackjack together in a room with the big boy aerospace industries who have already had historical antigravity contracts for ARVs for the past 6 decades. To get access to AG, the billionaires must ante-up or pony up to be a potential player and may the best rocket man win.

Lockheed Martin and Boeing has had AG subcontracts for ARVs since the 50's, but the billionaires are being played like a military con game to see who comes up with the best techno-designed rockets so the military can play the public con game with our TAX money for another 5 to 10 years. The military has to ultimately come clean about how they duped the American public like a crooked carnival barker before they open the flood gate to other private industries who already know the competitor bidding game. Given players are Lockheed Martin Marietta Skunk works, Raytheon, EG&G, Sandia Labs, and Motorola etc. the list goes on and on.

By then all the power broker generals and contractors will have played out the entire US treasury black project dollars to be given anyway. The US is so far in debt you might as well just start printing monopoly money with a UFO on one side and pick your favorite alien on the other. I don't doubt that some of the military brass and contractors have their own ARVs to go live on some other planet by that time and start their own colonies of remote earth establishments to see how much influence they can muster and wreak havoc with other alien civilizations.

Mosher, Graham Flanagan, Dave. n.d. "The Government Stopped Funding the Search for Aliens — and This Astronomer Says That's a Big Problem." Business Insider. Accessed June 8, 2023. https://www.businessinsider.com/nasa-search-intelligent-alien-life-seti-funding-2016-9.

updated, Richard Sammon last. 2013. "10 Ways Uncle Sam Wastes Your Tax Dollars." Kiplinger.com. May 31, 2013. https://www.kiplinger.com/slideshow/business/t043-s005-10-ways-uncle-sam-wastes-your-tax-dollars/index.html.

"1st Coordinated Green Bank Telescope/Allen Telescope Array Observes Possible Source of the WOW! Signal." n.d. SETI Institute. Accessed June 8, 2023. https://www.seti.org/1st-coordinated-green-bank-telescopeallen-telescope-array-observes-possible-source-wow-signal.

Even with all the negative NASA information above, NASA does get some recent extra credit for just launching a MARs mission with the largest rocket (Artemis) ever launched by NASA. Still this rocket is not necessary given that we have more advanced technology.

The US Government's Perspective:
The First Amendment states that "Congress shall make no law . . . abridging the freedom of speech," enforcement of political correctness in America normally comes not from legislation but from rules and regulations.

The Skeptic's Corner:
Yes, Mickey Mouse landed on the moon and visited the space station when he was an astronaut with NASA as we remember...

QUESTION 18:
Do we have simulators that teach our pilots to fly these ARV's we reversed engineered?

Tucker's Perspective:
Yes, Grand Bob told me that we have them.

The Fu Fu's Perspective:
We have multiple simulators built by existing aerospace contractors that help our pilots to fly AG craft or ARVs since 1958. According to Capt. Bill Uhouse, a former USAF/Army Air Corp fighter pilot, we have up to 36 reversed engineered antigravity craft designed from captured/crashed/acquired UFOs.

These Alien Reproduction Vehicles (ARV) work from (6) one-million-volt capacitors and 2 large deep cycle batteries. I believe his testimony is more than any other government official that has ever been in front of a microphone or before any congressional hearing.

Not only does Capt. Uhouse confirm we have these ARV aerospace craft graphic artist, but Mark McCandlish also confirms them as well.

The US Government's Perspective:
"Public realization that intelligent beings live on other planets could bring about profound changes, or even the collapse of our civilizations. Societies sure of their own place have disintegrated when confronted by a superior society". (1960 Brookings Institute research paper contracted by NASA.)

The Skeptic's Corner:

We have spent taxpayers' money to design simulators to help illegal aliens to scale our border walls, so they won't get hurt and I can give the little kids a hug and a Kiss. (Did Joe Biden say That?)

QUESTION 19:
Will all humans have to relearn basic history, biology, physics, and the history of civilization?

Tucker's Perspective:
I am learning it correctly for the first time from Grand Bob.

The Fu Fu's Perspective:
Yes, the short version is you can count on going back to school for another decade to catch up on remedial science, physics, and history unless the youth of America is told the truth about our ET friends and those other ETs who would like to eat us for dinner.

The smug Harvard types, the IVY League astronomers and SETI naysayers and all the other IVY leagues schools are tripping over themselves and rushing to get on the UFO Lecture Bandwagon Series to save face after helping the government for decades to demonize people like John Mack, MD and so many other so called "UFO conspiracy nuts". Now it's really the HAAVARRD types who get to be laughingstock kooks. MUFON is having the last laugh now.

Humans did not develop due to just evolution as Darwin had explained. Neither did earth's primitive life beginnings start by crawling out of a primordial soup of a neo-organic atmosphere with a helping porridge of amino acids with a touch of lightening as was taught in the Harvard, Yale, Sanford, and other IVY league colleges for the last 60 years.

"O Fantástico Relato de Bill Uhouse." n.d. Www.youtube.com. https://youtu.be/N_ZHujsRoo0.

"Zero Point the Story of Mark McCandlish and the Fluxliner 720p." n.d. Www.youtube.com. Accessed June 8, 2023. https://youtu.be/afLsRsd5roY.

Our entire academic lives as Baby Boomers have essentially been a stack of disinformation and have been secretly stolen from our timeline. Baby Boomers did not develop to their fullest potential due to a secretive government and complicit media and universities. At the same time, humans have been polluting the earth from technological ignorance that only a smidgen of the intelligence world were fully aware of our real options, even in the highest regarded academic circles.

It is almost comical if it weren't true that Sagan, Hynek with other famous astronomers. physicians and physicists on one hand were acting as genuine government lackeys debunking continuous reports by highly concerned citizens of valid UFO encounters. Their acts of debunking were rewarded with handouts of academic grants that funded their coveted post-doctoral programs and published academic drivel by comparison to ufologists, who are just now being taken seriously.

This approach by US government programs of discrediting and denial of public UFO contacts continued up until 2016 when Navy videos surfaced and were finally verified by the military. Coincidently, Dr. Hynek reversed himself, recognized the damage of his complicit role in the government coverup process and authored a book on Roswell (The Hynek UFO Report) that he tried to come clean.

As a testament, his son rose to the head of MUFON, a UFO supportive community who has attempted to correct the years of government disinformation. His son has multiple books at the core of his father's participation and what is being done currently to change that period of history.

And with a simple a touch of a sleight of hand these academics were also covertly contacted by our highly effective clandestine secretive government's special access programs to get nameless contracts from government intelligence agencies to investigate many parts of UFO wreckage, technology and non-terrestrial acquired evidence while destroying the lives of thousands of hard-working Americans who were just doing their duty and reporting the truth of their observations.

The real story that is told currently is seeds of other life landed here during earth's formation and ETs from other races have helped improve and tinker with human DNA and even the dinosaurs DNA as earth has been a giant petri dish for our alien parents. Earth's Garden of Eden could be called the Garden of Aliens.

The US Government's Perspective:
"Inflation is worse everywhere but here" …

The Skeptic's Corner:
On Man…You know our Inflation was all caused by Trump. (Joe Biden)

QUESTION 20:

Are there really Men In Black?

Tucker's Perspective:
Yes, I saw the Movie so it must be real.

The Fu Fu's Perspective:
Yes, there is a group of previous OSI agents who are now retired and classified as civilians who operate the Men In Black (MIB) Team in a Virginia AFB facility. These men in black go out and investigates UFO contacts or crashes where evidence of any type is not turned over to regular OSI officers and confiscated outright by any means.

If a UFO lands on your property, regular OSI agents have authority to confiscate and or seek a warrant to obtain and classify any or all your property as governmental property until they are satisfied your possessions or land does not pose any more of a risk to an investigation.

If the civilians are further resistant or are not cooperative with MIB, the MIB participates in covert programs and will secretly break into any residence or office to obtain the evidence. MIB has hired actors to even pose as pretend aliens and the witnesses are deceived and coerced to releasing any evidence. If the witness resist further with MIB even more drastic steps have been enacted in the past into giving up picture, video, even UFO wreckage, unearthly meta materials, or even alien body parts.

Many of the people who witnessed highly documented gifts from ETs, or witnessed UFOs with videos in the 50s, 60s, 70s and some of the 80s were contacted. After Digital cameras came out then the MIB teams would copy the real UFO add deliberate metadata changes that could be determines as fake and pass this disinformation off as real pictures to confuse the public as to the authenticity of the original picture.

The US Government's Perspective:

"Extraterrestrial life has never been discovered, but that doesn't mean it doesn't exist". NASA, astrobiologist, Lindsay Hays

The Skeptic's Corner:

If you think there are Men IN Black (MIB) coming to take away your UFOs in your backyard, then Men IN White (MIW) will be coming to take you away. (Ministry of Truth)

QUESTION 21:
Does the Art of Movie Making imitate life: Are Movies the Government's Tool of Disclosure?

Tucker's Perspective:

Yes, I have seen a lot of the TV shows on UFOs and ETs that Grand Bob watches. I like the ET movie.

The Fu Fu's Perspective:

Hollywood is the tool of our militaries for their excuse for soft disclosure. The US government wants to keep the ET/UFO technology secret but in the event, the government is forced to disclose secrets they will try and state the military created the science fiction "Star Trek" Phenomenon to soften disclosure. The USAF will ascribe to use that approach as a thinly veiled rationale excuse for mild public disclosure. Supposedly every space movie that has been successful in Hollywood regarding time travel, ET and UFOs came from real life events. The day the earth stood still MIB, ET the Extraterrestrial and Close encounters were from real life scripts with a bit of government and Hollywood tweaking.

Boeche, Dr Raymond W. n.d. "UFOs: Caught in a Web of Deception." Www.academia.edu. Accessed June 8, 2023. https://www.academia.edu/11583866/UFOs_Caught_in_a_Web_of_Deception.

I plan to continue using the word UFO and ARV not UAP until the government tells me and my grandson the truth about our ET neighbors and visitors of the universe. The head of Lockheed Skunk works, Ben Rich that developed the U2, SR-71 spy planes and are contractors for ARVs, stated, "We now have the technology to take ET home". I choose to believe him over our government any day of the week.

James Goodall, aerospace journalist and public speaker, became friends with Ben Rich. Goodall states that he spoke with Rich about 10 days before he died. The conversation took place over the phone while Rich was in the USC Medical Center in Los Angeles where Goodall claims that Rich said, "Jim, we have things out in the desert that are fifty years beyond what you can comprehend. If you have seen it on Star Wars or Star Trek, we've been there, done that, or decided it wasn't worth the effort. They have about forty-five hundred people at Lockheed Skunk Works. What have they been doing for the last 18 or 20 years? They're building something."

Virtually every successful ET Hollywood movie such as *Men In Black*, *Close Encounters of the Third Kind*, *ET*, and *When the Earth Stood Still* has been secretly co-scripted by obtained military/government consultants or CIA information found in various books or covertly leaked to movie script writers or movie studios.

Point in fact, the exchange program from Close Encounter of the Third Kind according to the movie was at Devils Tower, Wyoming which was an embellishment of an actual exchange in 1965 at Holloman AFB with an ET called an Extraterrestrial Biological Entity or EBENs and 12 of our astronauts. (There is a disagreement how many actual went, some documents say 10 went some documents say there were two females some documents say no females. One astronaut passed away in route to planet Serpo, two passed away on planet Serpo and one decided to stay on planet Serpo).

The mission was supposed to be over in ten years in 1975 but due to travel issues, the mission was extended. The 8 surviving astronauts returned to earth in 1978 and were sequestered for 7 years being debriefed. Even Gene Roddenberry was supposedly given actual scripts by the CIA based on actual exploits with our reverse engineered antigravity technology, our alien reproduction vehicles or ARVs and live ET visitors.

"The Lockheed Martin Director Who Publicly Commented on the SSP." N.d. Gaia. https://www.gaia.com/article/ben-rich-lockheed-martin-and-ufos.

The CIA have used the public to find out how well we would tolerate the concept that humans are not the smartest beings in the cosmos.

The US Government. During President Nixon's race for his second term in 1975, Nixon promised to release 16 minutes of an actual UFO landing at Holloman Airforce Base to Hollywood movie producer, Robert Emenegger for a UFO film documentary. UFOs: Past, Present, and Future is his 1974 documentary film. The producer was invited to Washington to see the video and was highly excited to obtain this footage and shared this with other production staff and directors.

This UFO landing was also witnessed firsthand and confirmed by Astronaut Gordon Cooper while he was an officer at that Air Force Base. Cooper also confirmed the film was immediately developed and then confiscated by military intelligence and flown to Washington.

On the day Robert Emenegger was supposed to obtain the footage by military courier, the release of the film was abruptly halted by President Nixon after the Watergate incident turned the opinion by his advisory staff on whether this material should be released to the public. Emenegger was shaken but went ahead with his 1974 documentary recreating the UFO landing incident accurately as per his viewing.

The US Government's Perspective:
We can't yet say for sure whether aliens exist. To quote Carl Sagan: "The universe is a big place. If it's just us, it seems like an awful waste of space." So, NASA will keep looking.

The Skeptic's Corner:
One day I think aliens will finally get here.

QUESTION 22:
Are many of our Air Force Bases (AFB) connected underground by tunnels to facilitate coordination of ET activities and military activities?

Tucker's Perspective:
Yes, I saw it on GAIA.TV or Ancient Aliens.

"Project Serpo: E.T. Exchange Program." N.d. Gaia. Accessed June 9, 2023. https://www.gaia.com/video/project-serpo-et-exchange-program.

The Fu Fu's Perspective:

Yes, supposedly many of our AFBs are connected underground from one end of our country (NC) to (Ca) along the entire 37th parallel. The host, Emory Smith of GAIA TV talks extensively about the tunnels. Paul Schneider, a government contract tunnel engineer gave many lectures of Tunnel wars with Aliens who made their tunnels that sometime conflicted with our tunnels & AFBs underground.

There is a 1974 patent for a giant nuclear tunnel boring machine (NTBM) that instantly fuses the ground rock and soil particles into solid reinforced braces as the machine is boring. This design eliminates the need to remove any byproducts of digging or pumping concrete into the construction site making this project totally hidden from satellites or ground observers.

Mr. Schneider stated supposedly 60 or more military, secret service and/or FBI personnel were lost in a massive gun battle that he participated in with underground aliens near Dulce AFB. He later mysteriously died and listed by the coroner as a suicide with a surgical tube wrapped around his neck. The Chinese, Russians and North Koreans have taken our lead and moved there sensitive miliary research development underground.

Talbert, Tricia. 2021. "Episode 5 – We Asked a NASA Scientist: Do Aliens Exist?" NASA. September 9, 2021. https://www.nasa.gov/feature/episode-5-we-asked-a-nasa-scientist-do-aliens-exist.

"'Something's Coming': Is America Finally Ready to Take UFOs Seriously?" 2022. The Guardian. February 5, 2022. https://www.theguardian.com/world/2022/feb/05/ufos-america-aliens-government-report.

The US Government's Perspective:
The Government will admit other drug cartels dig many tunnels into our borders to bring drugs that kills the US public.

The Skeptic's Corner:
No Way this happened. If you believe this, then I have a rare penny you can buy for a million dollars.

QUESTION 23:
What colors are the aliens and what colors, materials and shapes are their ET AG scout crafts or intergalactic ships?

AI Generated Art of various UFO shapes

Wang, Joshua Berlinger,Serenitie. 2018. "North Korea's Nuclear Test Caused Collapse, Study Says." CNN. April 26, 2018. https://www.cnn.com/2018/04/26/asia/north-korea-nuclear-test-site-punggye-ri-intl.

"ICYMI: ICE Discovers Sophisticated Subterranean Tunnel in California near U.S.-Mexico Border." 2021. Department of Homeland Security. August 11, 2021. https://www.dhs.gov/news/2021/08/11/icymi-ice-discovers-sophisticated-subterranean-tunnel-california-near-us-mexico.

Tucker's Perspective:

Shiny silver or grey.

The Fu Fu's Perspective:

The outside of most aliens' spaceships is dull silver, brushed aluminum or whiteish grey and most of the internal parts of the ship have very light grey uniformed colored features.

Linda Moulton Howe on Ancient Aliens TV series on The History Channel displayed a UFO "metamaterial" sample obtained given to her by a secret source who suggested it was a piece of actual alien craft wreckage he retrieved while serving in the military. The wreckage sample was tested at several metallurgical laboratories and tested as well on-air TV.

The sample was determined to be specific layers of metallic highly compressed material just nanometers thick of alternating zinc, bismuth and magnesium in a manner not found in any earth metal processing.

UFO shapes can be triangle, circular, cigar, oval egg, pyramid shapes changing from silver to black for space, even transparent for hiding and a mix of either silver for earth scout craft or black or white for RT drones. Several mass sightings in March 1997 in Phoenix, AZ, Texas, Ohio and New York, Hudson Valley saw a very, large black triangles 700 foot from one end of the triangle to the other in virtually any color to confuse our eyesight or blend in is used just as our military uses a similar approach with digital patterns confusing observers. Interdimensional ships can find their way past all physical obstacles and remain invisible, cloaked, appear as civilian aircraft and even 747s.

The Tall Whites have intergalactic ships that are black titanium and the smaller scout ships are white.

Our recent Tic Tac ships, ARV or AG drones are supposedly made in California Edwards Air force base at Lockheed Skunkworks Plant 42.

"S18e14 – Ancient Aliens on Location: The UFO Investigations – Ancient Aliens Transcripts – TvT." N.d. Accessed June 9, 2023. https://tvshowtranscripts.ourboard.org/viewtopic.php?f=1474&t=55957.

Banias, M. J. 2019. "UFO Researcher Explains Why She Sold 'Exotic' Metal to Tom DeLonge." Vice. November 14, 2019. https://www.vice.com/en/article/8xwp9z/ufo-researcher-explains-why-she-sold-exotic-metal-to-tom-delonge.

The US Government's Perspective:
Ronald Reagan told Americans in 1986, "We did not, I repeat, did not trade weapons or anything else [to Iran] for hostages, nor will we," four months before admitting that the U.S. had done what he had denied.

The Skeptic's Corner:
Oval rocks like flying saucers skip across the water best if you like to skip rocks.

QUESTION 24:
What does it smell like in an alien ship?

Tucker's Perspective:
Grand Bob said he read it smells like ozone, but I haven't smelled that before.

The Fu Fu's Perspective:
Yes, some of the examined craft have a distinctive smell that investigators have said is similar to ozone or a charged electric field in the air.

The US Government's Perspective:
White house staff is authorized to use only natural urinal cakes to make our bathrooms smell nice.

The Skeptic's Corner:
Ozone will kill a human if there is not oxygen present so that can't be the smell and anyway, there are no aliens.

QUESTION 25:
Does Russia Have a Similar military facility like Area 51 where UFO craft are studied?

Tucker's Perspective:
Yes, but I can't pronounce it.

US EPA, OAR. 2014. "Ozone Generators That Are Sold as Air Cleaners." Www.epa.gov. August 28, 2014. https://www.epa.gov/indoor-air-quality-iaq/ozone-generators-are-sold-air-cleaners#:~:text=Whether%20in%20its%20pure%20form

The Fu Fu's Perspective:

The Area is called Kapustin Yar. Much of ET research and many UFOs that Russia has retrieved or shot down are taken to Kapustin Yar. On one event in the 80's a cigar shaped antigravity craft was shot down and the 4 aliens were captured and held in a concrete detention center and 24 hours later that had been teleported out of their prison by their aliens. American spy network that had infiltrated the Russian Military base confirmed this event.

China has acquired UFO/ET technology by, retrieval of alien craft in their country, spying/counterintelligence with its network of spies in the US, in our military and in NASA in 2021. The Chinese have also attempted to infiltrate and steal research from aerospace business and technical colleges.

AI Generated Art of Kapustin Yar

Reuters. 2021. "NASA Scientist Pleads Guilty to Lying about China Ties," January 13, 2021, sec. APAC. https://www.reuters.com/article/us-usa-china-nasa-plea/nasa-scientist-pleads-guilty-to-lying-about-china-ties-idUSKBN29I345.

Nast, Condé. 2022. "Have Chinese Spies Infiltrated American Campuses?" The New Yorker. March 11, 2022. https://www.newyorker.com/magazine/2022/03/21/have-chinese-spies-infiltrated-american-campuses.

The US Government's Perspective:

We need to confront people in restaurants and where they live (CA:Maxine Waters) We need to close (burn) down police stations, dismantle and defund the police.

The Skeptic's Corner:

Russia doesn't let any illegal aliens in their country as opposed to the US (Putin)

CHAPTER 10
ON ALIEN ABDUCTIONS…

The possibility of extraterrestrial encounters or abductions indeed stirs the imagination. I've tried to impart this wisdom on ETs and UFOs. When it comes to this matter, as one ventures into the solitude of the wilderness, one must cast their gaze upwards, for the celestial expanse might offer more than simply avian and cloud spectacles.

There are numerous accounts, each a narrative imbued with a sense of the unknown. The incident involving Barney and Betty Hill, for instance, presents a compelling narrative. The tale has even permeated popular culture, as represented by the film adaptation of Communion. Travis Walton's account is equally fascinating. A logger by trade, Walton reportedly vanished for a full five days, his entire crew maintaining that he had been whisked away by an unidentifiable beam of light.

In Pascagoula, Mississippi, a pair of fishermen made a claim of abduction, and there's the distressing narrative of Sgt. Lovette, who was found horrifically mutilated subsequent to a UFO sighting. This event so traumatized his partner, Major Cunningham, that it led to a significant mental break. Tales of similar encounters have even emerged from as far away as Nome, Alaska, though the veracity of these accounts remains a topic of debate.

Numerous other encounters have been reported, some substantiated by multiple witnesses. Notable among these are the Rendlesham Forest incident in the United Kingdom, and the occurrence at Ramstein Air Force Base. One particular incident involved a soldier developing a heart condition following a UFO sighting, which required the intervention of Senator McCain to secure the necessary medical attention.

There's the intriguing case of Raymond Powtroisky, a civilian who resided in proximity to the Dugway Proving Grounds. According to reports, he established a friendship with a 7-foot-tall extraterrestrial being and was even invited inside his egg-shaped craft. Before his demise, Powtroisky was allegedly the recipient of various gifts from his alien friend, leaving these artifacts to Rick Doty and the Air Force.

The larger question remains, are these visitors from other realms merely observing us, or do they intend to leave tangible evidence of their visits? Is their purpose to bestow upon us mementos, knowledge, or merely narratives for our collective folklore? As I ponder these questions, I recall a recent news feature on the Today Show, a report of a former fighter pilot who sighted a UFO near the Big Dipper constellation. Indeed, we live in a world filled with curiosity and wonder.

CHAPTER 11
HOW UFOS CONNECTED TO THE PYRAMIDS AROUND THE WORLD

Recently, in a February 2023 episode of the 20th season of GAIA TV, Rick Doty confirmed some extraordinary insights about the pyramids globally. He shared that the 1947 Roswell crash and the subsequent discovery of the Extraterrestrial Biological Entity 1 (EBE 1) provided unique insights into the mysteries surrounding the pyramids.

EBE 1 was placed under the surveillance of a military captain, serving as a 24-hour handler. With a specially designed vibrational voice box, EBE 1 was able to translate its alien sounds into rudimentary yet comprehensible English. During their conversations, EBE 1 divulged secrets about the pyramids that remain unknown or unacknowledged by many academic Egyptian pyramid experts.

Egypt, with over 118 pyramids, is known to have several of these structures built with the cooperation of humans and extraterrestrial beings, as documented by the CIA. Pyramids worldwide, many in various states of disrepair, have also been linked to extraterrestrial origins by our intelligence agencies.

The US government has been conducting intensive research on pyramids since the 1930s, preceding WWII. During the war, Germany also sent teams to investigate these structures for potential energy sources. It was discovered that many pyramids generate basic electronic frequency signals.

In the 1950s, following WWII, the CIA dispatched covert investigative teams into the pyramids. Equipped with signal collectors, these teams discovered hundreds of frequencies emanating from within. With more advanced signal collection devices, later investigations throughout the late 1950s, 1960s, and in 1981 found advanced signals in the Gigahertz range.

EBE 1 confirmed that the pyramids serve multiple functions, and were constructed across the globe through the combined efforts of extraterrestrials and various ancient civilizations:

1. Pyramids were constructed globally and on other planets to serve as navigational beacons. They generate frequencies, notably in the Gigahertz range, much like the VOR ADF navigation system used by aircraft. These signals guide ET crafts navigating the Earth and are not necessarily used for interstellar travel.

2. Pyramids can generate power, to the extent that some have reportedly recharged batteries. Alien crafts have been known to recharge their energy reserves at these sites. This is achieved by channeling Earth's magnetic power and ions into an energy field. Unfortunately, the original Giza pyramids have lost this ability due to the erosion of their shiny, white limestone coating.

3. Pyramids were also used for healing. Artifacts discovered by CIA teams were found to possess healing properties, only activated within the pyramid structures.

4. Some artifacts retrieved from the pyramids were proven to be of extraterrestrial origin. Their unique metallurgical composition and elements not found on Earth confirmed their alien nature. Extraterrestrial skeletons have also been discovered near pyramids worldwide, verified by CIA pathologists and other global experts such as Dr. Kit Green, a known former CIA contract research physician.

5. EBE 1 stated that the sand from the pyramids in Egypt and the Middle East possesses healing properties.

6. It is speculated that underground water reservoirs contribute to some pyramidal powers.

7. Most strikingly, several pyramids were found to contain portals to other dimensions, confirmed by CIA research teams who experienced time displacement. Despite some teams disappearing momentarily into these dimensions, no teams have been lost. These phenomena have also been extensively researched by Dr. Harold "Hal" Puthoff, an American contract CIA researcher.

8. The ubiquitous 'Watchful Eye' symbol found in many pyramids and structures represents extraterrestrial beings monitoring Earth and the universe.

EBE 1 ultimately died but he confirmed the above information.

In 1991 research teams digging through the Egyptian pyramids and Great Sphinx into never exposed tunnels and large rooms found a small 4-foot lethargic ET with a triangle Egyptian headdress like Egyptian pharaohs was supposedly found inside a newly excavated chamber with no food or water for 5000 years existing solely on the energy made by the pyramid. The ET told the teams he was the guardian of that pyramid. No other information was attributed to whether he was recovered or if he disappeared, but it was confirmed by several UIS and German research teams his presence was real.

I highly recommend you listen to the multitude of Rick Doty GAIA Interviews to learn more about these subjects.

Antarctica Pyramids

In a recent GAIA TV interview, Doty discussed the discovery of ancient pyramids in Antarctica. He elaborated on a particular incident from 1999 when a 15-foot diameter, 50-foot-long extraterrestrial (ET) craft was found near one of these pyramids. The craft, believed to be buried under ice for several thousand years, was still powered and lit up beneath the ice. Following its discovery, it was transported to Area 51 for further study.

The craft's discovery came decades after two directed energy weapon tests – "Project Spartan" in 1976 and "Project Zeus" in 1978. These tests reportedly sent energy beams into a half-mile tunnel, leading to the creation of an opening to a large cavern by 1981. This cavern, upon exploration, revealed an underground pyramid. Initial entry into the cavern led to the discovery of a toxic green algae that threatened the research team.

Subsequent explorations were conducted with appropriate protective gear. The cavern itself was illuminated by a green light emanating from the walls and ceiling, with no obvious or conventional light sources.

Doty also shared accounts from several expeditions to Antarctica made by volunteer Air Force polar air transport teams. They reported large openings, from which UFOs were seen entering and exiting, in the Antarctic ice. As a result, these teams have been ordered to avoid flying over or near these openings. Multiple Air Force teams and SEAL personnel, assigned to recover unknown objects and research personnel from Antarctica, have confirmed these observations.

The historical records indicate that the Germans conducted numerous expeditions to Antarctica both before and during World War II. These records reveal that the Nazis transported massive amounts of rail and housing equipment to Antarctica and used imported machinery to generate steam, creating igloo-like caverns beneath the ice glaciers for heat conservation. They even brought in children and female psychologists to investigate "alternative realities". The Nazis claimed to have discovered portals to other dimensions, similar to those reported near pyramid sites worldwide. The presence of German activity in Antarctica was also confirmed by Admiral Byrd and research teams in 1991.

In 2015, Doty mentioned, there were delegations of senior Vatican personnel and politicians from the US, Canada, Germany, and other European countries who visited the underground pyramid. The purpose of the visit was to validate the existence of these ET technologies and to secure multinational funding for further research. Reports of these visits were subsequently leaked and confirmed by UFO researchers.

This information aligns with the insights shared by our ET visitor, EBE 1, a survivor from the 1947 Roswell Crash, and is further corroborated by several decades of research led by the CIA and DIA.

The Dark Black Alaskan Pyramid

In UFO lore, a particularly intriguing story, corroborated by two separate military intelligence officers from the Army and the Air Force, revolves around a 200-acre tract of land located a few miles west of Denali National State Park's boundary. This area, which is strictly off-limits to all non-military personnel, is said to house an underground "Black" or Dark

Pyramid. This structure, completely buried and standing 540 feet tall, is surrounded by a large cavern that is reportedly overseen by both the US military and extraterrestrial entities (ETs) working together. Their joint effort aims to maintain this pyramid, perceived as a galactic refueling station, for visiting extraterrestrial ships.

The intelligence officers stated that the pyramid serves as a unique energy refilling station for UFOs. It draws energy from the Earth and transmits it directly above to waiting UFOs from various parts of the galaxy. This pyramid, which has purportedly been in operation for hundreds of thousands of years, is the tallest in the world, standing one hundred feet taller than the Pyramid of Giza. The Dark Pyramid allegedly functions in a manner similar to other pyramids across the Earth, historically tapping into energy for rendezvous with alien vessels. This suggests that past civilizations were not only aware of these pyramids' purposes but also actively assisted the alien cultures.

CHAPTER 12
ON ALIEN POLITICS AND WHY THE US GOVERNMENT WILL NOT SHARE ALIEN TECHNOLOGY

Now listen here, my dear friends. I've spent a fair share of my years navigating the complexities of this world, and I've learned a thing or two in my time, particularly when it comes to the dance of power and how it affects us all. In my position as an educated man, as a physician who's seen the many facets of life, I'd like to discuss something that's been occupying my thoughts of late - the politics of extraterrestrials, or to be more specific, why our U.S. government might be reluctant to share what I've come to call Acquired Advanced Alien Technology (AAAT) if you will.

However, our U.S. government is built upon a different paradigm. It desires to maintain its power structure, its influence over citizens' choices, its control over energy grids, borders, and space, its authority over financial systems and taxation. The possession and control of advanced weapons for protection also falls under this domain. I am sure you can see the friction here.

And then there are we, the individuals, who yearn for freedom of choice, free energy technology, advanced travel, and the opportunity to earn our own keep without excessive taxation. We also seek the right to protect ourselves and, perhaps most importantly, we long for the ability to expand our consciousness.

ET Aliens Have	US Government Wants	Individuals Want
Unlimited control over others	Power over citizens choices	Freedom of Choice
Unlimited Free Energy	Power from the energy grid	Free energy technology
Unlimited interstellar travel	Power over borders/space	Freedom of Advanced travel
Cashless society/Barter/favors	Power over Financial/Commerce	Freedom to make money
Taxless society	Power for taxation	Less taxes the better
Advanced weapons for protection	Nuclear weapons for protection	Guns for protection
Expanded Advanced Consciousness	Limits over Consciousness	Wants to Expand Consciousness

Now, I don't say this with surprise or judgement. It's simply the reality of the world we live in. I'm sure our government is concerned that if they were to introduce advanced alien technology, they could potentially lose the structure they've carefully built. If citizens were given access to such advancements, it could possibly liberate us from governmental constraints, reduce our need for taxation, and even expand our consciousness. I suppose you could say the fear is that they might not be able to contain us. But after all, isn't growth and advancement what we all strive for? As we age and gain wisdom, we begin to see that progress often comes with a certain level of commotion. Perhaps it's time we start embracing that.

CHAPTER 13
THE HIDDEN TRUTH: EXTRATERRESTRIAL EXISTENCE AND ITS IMPACT ON AMERICA'S FUTURE

In the United States, there's a broad cross-section of individuals who possess knowledge about extraterrestrials (ETs) and unidentified flying objects (UFOs). This includes all the presidents who have served in office, with varying levels of briefings on the subject. Many military intelligence agencies, along with certain government entities, are also privy to this information.

The American populace's awareness of ETs and UFOs is wide-ranging. According to various American polls, anywhere from 34 to 65 percent of the public believe in their existence. This implies that out of the total U.S. population of approximately 337 million, as many as 225,790,000 people are believers. This is largely attributable to widespread access to television, which has facilitated the dissemination of previously top-secret military videos showcasing supersonic jet gun camera footage of tic-tac UFOs, gimbal UFOs, go-fast UFOs, and those seen diving underwater or entering and exiting volcanoes. These visuals present convincing evidence of extraterrestrial craft to all but the most skeptical or uninformed viewers.

Interestingly, an estimated four million alien abductees reside within the U.S. Moreover, about 20,000 UFO sighting reports are filed by observers annually, suggesting that approximately 20 million people have seen UFOs. It's worth noting that this figure excludes the roughly 1,000 individuals too anxious to admit their encounters.

Members of the Mutual UFO Network (MUFON), Sirius Disclosure,

Earth Files, and various other UFO/ET groups, are undoubtedly convinced of the existence of these phenomena. These memberships account for about one million additional fervent believers.

However, it's worth highlighting the paradoxical fact that the information related to advanced scientific discoveries of new physics, aerospace, and energy power sources, remains a closely guarded secret. Only around 2,000 individuals in intelligence and top-secret Special Access Program (SAP) government contractors, who are involved in reverse engineering Alien Reproduction Vehicles (ARVs) and advanced energy platforms, have this knowledge. This means a minuscule .00000059 percent of the American public have access to these groundbreaking revelations.

Such restrictions seem unfair considering the potential benefits of this technology. It could make our world safer, stronger, and allow for the use of superior, pollution-free energy sources, thus replacing antiquated polluting technologies. Furthermore, the implications of this technology could fundamentally alter our relationship with space. The ability to explore the universe, asteroid belts, and planetary bodies without rockets could revolutionize our resource gathering methods, easing the strain on Earth's resources.

This transition could lead to a reduction in global military posturing, fostering an era of cooperation and shared resources. It is time for those holding this powerful knowledge, many of whom have families, to step up and share it for the betterment of mankind. Otherwise, we run the risk of remaining under the control of a minuscule fraction of our military and private government contractors, a situation which denies us access to advanced science and the truth we deserve. The filmmaker Steven Spielberg once mused about these UFOs: "What if it's us, 500,000 years in the future?" This conjecture merely highlights the myriad of possibilities we stand to uncover by seeking the truth about ETs and UFOs.

CHAPTER 14
FROM UNDERSTANDING TO ACTION: ENGAGING WITH THE UFO AND ET PHENOMENA

This book presents three key actions to understand and apply the immense volume of UFO and ET knowledge.

First, exercise your democratic rights by contacting your US Congressional Representative or US Senator. Request them to invite individuals like Rick Doty, Dr. Greer, and Bob Lazar who have experience with ET/UFO investigations to testify before Congress. This act can spark transparency and disclosure.

Second, emphasize the importance of government truthfulness. It's crucial to grant legislative immunity to government witnesses, allowing them to breach their Non-Disclosure Agreements. Advocate for Rick Doty's participation in the Congressional Interview process, unveiling the complexities to the public. This could prompt military brass into revealing deeper truths to protect their post-retirement aerospace industry jobs.

Third, ensure the safety of witnesses like Rick Doty from potential harm by government-associated elements. Anyone with Doty's intelligence could be a target. Our government has a history of clandestine operations, particularly when exposed to criticism and the unveiling of falsehoods.

To delve further into UFOs and ETs, consider some reliable information sources. Start with Dr. Greer's website, www.siriusdisclosure.com, and explore the testimonials. Join www.GAIA.com to watch Richard Doty's interviews and visit www.Earthfiles.com for Linda Moulton Howe's podcasts. Cable TV's 'Ancient Aliens' and YouTube offer abundant UFO-related content. For a more in-depth understanding, read works by Dr. Greer, Charles J. Hall, and Linda Moulton Howe's 'A Strange Harvest'. Lastly, www.Exopolitics.com frequently offers substantial information on ETs and UFOs. However, maintain a healthy skepticism throughout your research.

On June 12, 2023, Dr. Greer hosted an event at the National Press Club in Washington D.C., where four highly credible, thoroughly vetted whistleblowers came forward. These individuals shared their extraordinary experiences with Unidentified Flying Objects (UFOs) during their military service, shedding light on the extent of government cover-ups. Notably, this event was not covered by any major news outlets.

In the final hour of this three-hour event, Dr. Greer introduced a lawyer who announced he had rallied a team of 90 other attorneys. Their plan was to leverage the Racketeer Influenced and Corrupt Organizations (RICO) Act in order to prosecute the government and military contractors, whom they allege have been disseminating disinformation about UFOs for the past 80 years. This represents a significant effort to unveil the truth about UFOs.

In an exceptional revelation, Richard Doty shared the extraordinary story of Cady Smith on GAIA TV on 6/13/23. Cady, half alien, and half human was contracted as an OSI agent by the Airforce. Accepting the existence of UFOs and ETs leads to the realization that these aliens have assimilated among us, through various means like shape-shifting and covert alien-human hybrid abduction programs. Cady's story suggests that these **aliens might even vote**. Curiously, it remains unknown which political party these aliens prefer.

There are significant developments in the sphere of Unidentified Flying Objects (UFOs) and Extraterrestrial (ET) events. The 2023 defense bill, endorsed by a bipartisan majority, includes a section proposed by the Republican-led House of Representatives that offers protection to former intelligence officers, military personnel, government employees, and private contractors involved in special access programs concerning classified UFO/ET events.

The newly approved defense bill permits any individual who has signed a Non-Disclosure Agreement (NDA) related to Top Secret Sensitive

Compartmented Information (TS/SCI), a classification level above top secret, to legally disregard the NDA and reveal any information as a protected whistleblower concerning government secrecy on UFO/ET matters. In the past month, five individuals have already come forward, and this is likely just the beginning as others are observing from the sidelines.

However, one major concern is that not all potential whistleblowers will be able to testify before Congress. In the past, some UFO witnesses who attempted to come forward encountered mysterious, sudden fatalities. The knowledge humanity will gain from this substantial congressional effort to conduct UFO hearings remains to be seen. It is my hope that this book will help you, the reader, quickly understand this crucial technological and intellectual matter, and contribute to a world that is safer, healthier, and overall better.

"UFO/UAP Disclosure Press Conference." 2023. National Press Club. 2023. https://www.press.org/events/ufouap-disclosure-press-conference.

"Monday, June 12, 2023! Dr. Greer's Groundbreaking National Press Club Event! FREE to Watch!" n.d. Www.youtube.com. Accessed June 21, 2023. https://www.youtube.com/live/zDY7t6HihCw?app=desktop.

EPILOGUE

The journey is far from its conclusion. Tucker and I maintain our vigil, our eyes ever skyward, with a mixture of curiosity and anticipation. We do hope that the echo of your voices, through letters and phone calls, reaches the ears of your representatives, compelling them to summon verifiable experts - individuals with firsthand governmental employment track records. People like Richard Doty or Bob Lazar, or those who have experienced the inexplicable, akin to Dr. Greer. The likes of Travis Walton, too, who bear testament to unorthodox abductions. Their testimonies are crucial to enlighten the American public about our quiet, unacknowledged role as terrestrial hosts to extraterrestrial visitors and their vessels.

Since 1947, US citizens have been unwittingly financing an Alien Hootenanny Celebration, an 80 yearlong affair, through their hard-earned tax dollars. Regrettably, the US government has overlooked inviting the real stakeholders - the taxpayers, individuals like you and me.

Perhaps, in the near future, hotels like the Marriott or Holiday Inn might offer special rates for our varied extraterrestrial guests, saving them the inconvenience of a stay in USAF military barracks. Imagine a MUFON conference where the guest speakers are authentic Alien Visitors!

Tucker and I stand ready to facilitate this event, our doors wide open for enriching telepathic conversations and vegetarian extraterrestrial cracker dinners with our galactic compatriots. These esteemed guests are welcome to park their vehicles in our backyard, draw water from our pond, and even proudly display their ray guns on our premises. ***Stay Tuned!***

APPENDIX

Prominent Figures in Ufology

Please note that the information contained in this appendix is based on research up until the year 2023. It is always important to continue to seek out the most current information, as new discoveries, developments, and perspectives continue to emerge in this ever-evolving field.

This section discusses notable investigative journalists, reporters, UFO authors, and ufologists who have contributed significantly to our understanding of unidentified flying objects (UFOs) and extraterrestrial (ET) life. For many years, academic institutions and the wider scientific community largely dismissed the study of UFOs. However, following the release of military footage and other supporting materials in 2017, this field has gained more mainstream acceptance.

Notable figures include:

Erich von Däniken: A Swiss born writer and one of the most widely known published historical authors of all human history and Ufology who wrote the book, Chariots of Fire in 1968. Eric Von Daniken was one of the first persons to connect the world history of UFOs to world religions and present a new understanding of human ancient history. Von Daniken was the absolute scourge of every academic institution in the world who could not bear to have their authority challenged on world religion and human history. Von Daniken is the first to rewrite human history and is still waiting on academic institutions to apologize for their ignorance on the subject. Currently most of the "notable" academic institutions and astrobiologists are now tripping over each other to announce that UFOs are now real after 80 years of institutionalized disinformation.

Linda Moulton Howe: One of the longest known UFO investigative reporters and first to report on UFO related cattle mutilations and author on the first book called, A Strange Harvest Author on cattle mutilations and UFO investigator who has over 50 years' experience. Has a regular monthly podcast called Earthfiles.com has the largest repository of UFO related stories in the world and has been featured on more TV documentaries, TV shows and News reports than any other female ufologist. She feels that UFOs are friendly and could have wiped us out long ago if they were all of a hostile origin but admits that human abductions and cattle mutilations are part of the aliens.

Leslie Keen: Long time investigative Journalist on the UFO subject for over 30 years. Was able to get UFO stories printed in newspapers when other journalists were not. Broke the US Air Force video releases in 2017 story through the NY Times. Wrote a book in 2011 on UFOs called UFOs and has been featured in numerous UFO documentaries, TV shows and Podcasts. She does subscribe to the fact UFOs are a military threat to the US airspace to advance her UFO stories as does the NYT to appease the military's narrative for more funding. Up until 2017 the NYT along with other newspapers were paid to not run stories on UFOs or discredit UFO witnesses that came forward to inform the public.

Bill Birnes: Publisher of UFO Magazine, TV personality of the TV series UFO Hunters, Unsealed: Aliens Files and extensive ufologist podcasts. Author of 25 books including UFOs and the Paranormal. Extensively quoted and featured in many UFO conferences.

Richard Dolan: Investigative Reporter and author who has extensive discussions on TV documentaries such as Ancient Aliens, other UFO series and podcasts. Richard Dolan is among the world's leading UFO researchers, historians, and publishers. He has written four groundbreaking books. These include two volumes of history, UFOs and the National Security State, an analysis of the future,

Nick Pope: Former staff member of the UK Ministry of Defense assigned to the "UFO Desk". Has extensive government secrecy clearances with the UK and investigated numerous UFO events in the British government. UFO researcher and numerous TV documentary series such as Ancient Aliens and national TV broadcasts and podcasts. Published Open Skies, Closed Minds.

Travis Taylor: Astrophysicist, former NASA researcher, former of the US DIA UAP task force has appeared on numerous UFO TV series such as Skinwalker Ranch and Ancients Aliens.

Giorgio A. Tsoukalos: is a Swiss-born writer, and television presenter and producer. He is a ufologist and a promoter of the ancient astronaut's hypothesis. He is best known for his appearances on Ancient Aliens, a History Channel series of which he is also a producer.

Andrew Collins: Author of numerous books on multiple subjects regarding UFOs and ETs as they relate to ancient history and religion. Frequent appearance on the TV show Ancient Aliens.

Encounter Stories

UFO hit with Snowball: In 1979, Bruce Manley reported seeing a UFO from his home in Kasilof, Alaska. One night, after returning home late from work on an oil rig, Manley was relaxing in his living room when he noticed multicolored lights moving down the river behind his house. He went outside and saw a triangular craft moving slowly about 20 feet above the river at eye level, around 25 feet long and 20 feet wide.

As the silent craft glided by, Manley felt compelled to grab some snow and throw a snowball at it. The snowball struck the UFO, but it did not react and continued moving down the river until it went out of sight. Manley's account was featured on the TV show Aliens in Alaska.

UFO experts now believe the Johnston Atoll Air Force Base and U.S. Wildlife Research Park acts as an intermittent base and meeting point for an interstellar federation from 574 planets. The base has expanded with no public visibility or access unless specially permitted by the Air Force.

Rumor has it the Air Force and Defense Intelligence Agency have handed oversight of past alien activity and historical records to the new U.S. Space Force. A four-star Space Force general has said the Force received a $3 million payout from the FBI to censor conservatives on Twitter four months before the 2020 election.

The FBI also hid information on Hunter Biden three weeks before the election. The government claimed five Capitol Police officers were killed during the January 6, 2021, protests at the Capitol, but no officers actually died from violence that day. One officer died of a stroke the next day, unrelated to injuries. The only protester shot was an unarmed woman killed by a Capitol Police officer. Three other protesters died of medical issues.

Now that Elon Musk has shown Twitter illegally conspired with the FBI to censor not just Republicans but moderate Democrats and scientific information countering the official COVID-19 narrative, it is clear the government also worked with Facebook and Google to suppress conservative ideas, erase factual history, and spread misinformation. For nearly 100 years, this censorship has been used to spread disinformation about UFOs. Facebook and Google have promoted extreme liberal ideologies, gender propaganda, and critical race theory to children with government support.

Speed of light is too Slow: According to Dr. Steven Greer, consciousness is not limited by the speed of light. Consciousness is essentially instantaneous and can travel infinitely fast, enabling communication with alien civilizations and humanoids light years away, as quantum entanglement shows. When people pray or meditate, their consciousness connects instantly with God, not limited by the speed of light. Understanding consciousness is key to understanding space travel.

Greer says private military contractors secretly run the UFO program, creating hybrid aliens and anti-gravity craft to stage an invasion. There are unacknowledged Special Access Programs beyond government control researching UFOs and aliens. Presidents cannot access Area 51, and only Nixon, Reagan, and select military leaders knew the full truth. Exposing these secrets would require attacking our own military.

26 Solar Systems: According to Linda Moulton Howe's contacts and whistleblowers, in a 2022 interview on GAIA TV and from her website, Earthfiles.com, astronauts from the US newly created Space Force and the current Air Force have traveled to 26 solar systems as guests on the space crafts used by the Nordics and Tall White aliens. All these alternate solar systems are up to 15 light years aways but in these alien craft is that less than a day and a half in earth time through advanced flight and portal technology.

If this information is true, the government uses the Hubble and James Webb telescopes to slowly release information about potentially habitable exoplanets, though astronauts have allegedly visited 26-star systems with alien craft. For 70 years, the government has spread misinformation with media help. When one party is in power, government overreach is limited; when the other is in power, legal standards are ignored to expand control. Disclosure may unite people once we learn the truth: extraterrestrials have been on Earth for ages.

Until the Nordics, Tall Whites and the Greys start selling tickets for space rides to the average US citizen Joe or Jill to explore the solar system, we still will be drip fed this non-ET gobbledygook we have been nursing from our government until the onion layers are peeled away so far back, the government starts to critically hemorrhage the rushing truth.

Whistleblowers and Insiders

This section presents information shared by individuals who risked their lives and reputations to shed light on UFOs and ET life. These figures include:

Richard Doty: retired Air Force special agent: Richard Doty served for over eight years with the Air Force Office of Special Investigations (AFOSI), investigating UFO sightings and events at Kirkland AFB and Area 51. Doty has gone on the record with many details of his work obtaining materials from crashed UFOs, interrogating EBEs, and attempting to back-engineer alien technology. He testifies that we have developed antigravity propulsion, new energy sources, and more from studying ET craft. Doty represents one of the highest-ranking government whistleblowers to come forward with direct experience handling UFO-related topics.

Bob Lazar: whistleblower who exposed Area 51: Bob Lazar was employed at Area 51's Site 4, known as S-4, in 1988 and 1989. While working there, he witnessed nine color-coded flying saucers of extraterrestrial origin at the base. Lazar has provided detailed accounts of how these craft operate using antigravity propulsion powered by element 115. His testimony made Area 51's existence public and has been partially corroborated by others. Skeptics attempt to discredit Lazar, but many researchers find him credible based on the accuracy of his claims.

Capt. Bill Uhouse, retired Air Force pilot who test flew ARVs: Capt. Bill Uhouse was an engineer and test pilot for the Air Force who claimed our government possesses at least three alien reproduction vehicles (ARVs), reverse-engineered from crashed UFOs, that he personally flew at Edwards AFB. Uhouse described the ARVs as using a capacitor system and having a generator that distorts time and space. He said the craft could reach the moon in minutes and that we have had this technology since the 1950s. Uhouse believed disclosure was long overdue. His testimony confirms other reports of man-made UFO-type craft used in secret space programs.

Emery Smith: whistleblower with experience at underground bases: Emery Smith is a former USAF subcontractor who has come forward about his work at underground biotech research facilities related to UFO and ET materials. Smith claims to have autopsied more than 3,000 extraterrestrial biological entities (EBEs) and participated in Project Moon Shadow, helping to recover UFO craft including the Roswell wreckage. While criticized by some, Smith's detailed accounts of underground bases and ETs coincide with other whistleblower reports, and he has shared photos, documents, and artifacts as evidence to support his claims.

Charles J. Hall: whistleblower who had contact with the "Tall Whites": Charles Hall was an enlisted man in the USAF who served at Indian Springs in Nevada. While there, he claimed to have interactions with a group of ETs called the "Tall Whites" as part of an exchange program. Hall described them as humanoid but albino, about 6-9 feet tall and curious toward human groups. He said the USAF provided infrastructure for the Tall Whites in exchange for technological information, including data used to develop fiber optics, night vision, and the atomic bomb. Hall's accounts are controversial, but he is considered an important figure in ufology and the study of secret programs related to UFOs.

Dr. Steven Greer: founder of the Disclosure Project: Dr. Greer is an emergency room physician who founded the Center for the Study of Extraterrestrial Intelligence (CSETI) and The Disclosure Project. Greer researches UFO and ET phenomena, claiming we have made contact with several civilizations that wish to share knowledge and technology but are forbidden by illegal government secrecy and programs. Greer works to end UFO secrecy and bring disclosure of classified technologies that could eliminate pollution and poverty. He has provided a platform for hundreds of government witnesses to come forward with testimony about ET contact, secret programs, and exotic propulsion technologies.

Alien Abductions

Reports of alien abductions and human experimentation have been reported and, in some cases, verified through implants, scarring, or post-traumatic stress disorder (PTSD) among the victims. Notable cases include those of Barney and Betty Hill, Whitley Strieber, and Travis Walton. Although proving these cases definitively can be challenging, the similarities in the details reported by various victims suggest a physical or interdimensional phenomenon.

Government and defense contractors such as Lockheed Martin, Northrop Grumman, and Boeing Aerospace, among others, reportedly participate in secretly funded Special Access Programs (SAPs). These programs, managed by the Defense Advanced Research Projects Agency (DARPA), involve activities like reverse engineering or antigravity propulsion of alien Special Reversed Engineered (ARV) non-human spacecraft, ARVonics (alien flight controls), security enforcement of antigravity programs, or the storage of meta-materials from alien spacecraft.

Notable Alien Abductions:

Travis Walton was reportedly abducted by a UFO on November 5, 1975, with his logging crew witnessing the event. He returned five days later, severely dehydrated. Polygraph tests confirmed the legitimacy of the crew's account, and the event was later adapted into a book and movie, 'Fire in the Sky.' Philip J. Klass, an American journalist and UFO researcher and renowned for his skeptical stance towards the existence of extraterrestrial phenomena, is featured in a Larry King Live episode about Walton.

In Pascagoula, Mississippi, two fishermen claimed to be abducted by robot-like aliens. Their accounts were deemed credible by local authorities and their experience received wide media attention.

In 1956, Sgt. Lovette was allegedly abducted by a UFO at White Sands Missile Range, confirmed by radar data and Major Cunningham's testimony. His mutilated body was found three days later, ten miles from the site.

"Larry King Live – Walton UFO Abduction Case (3/12/1993)." n.d. Www.youtube.com. https://www.youtube.com/watch?v=6G1LTErasps.

"1975 Interview with a Man Who Claims He Was Abducted by Aliens." n.d. Www.youtube.com. https://www.youtube.com/watch?v=SjlzeYiGLzc.

"Alien Contact: The Pascagoula UFO Encounter (FULL MOVIE)." n.d. Www.youtube.com. https://www.youtube.com/watch?v=4Q94ythKR5A.

Speculations regarding the Nome, Alaska, ET abductions and UFOs are an adaptation of the movie "The Fourth Kind." This event is speculative.

Significant ET/UFO/ARV Contact Events:

Intriguing ET/UFO/ARV contact events include the Rendlesham Forest incident in the UK, the Kecksburg incident in Pennsylvania, the Berwyn Mountain UFO incident in Wales, the Lonnie Zamora incident in New Mexico, the Phoenix Lights event in Arizona, the Hudson Valley UFO Event Series in New York, and more.

Notably, the Rendlesham Forest incident involved multiple soldiers witnessing contact with a 9-foot black triangle. The Kecksburg incident involved a bell-shaped UFO being recovered by the military while being watched by locals. The Phoenix Lights event was a mass UFO sighting witnessed by over 10,000 people in Phoenix and Henderson, Nevada.

Other significant contact events include the O'Hare Airport UFO sighting in Chicago, the Aurora Texas UFO crash, reported UFO experiences by former Presidents Thomas Jefferson and George Washington, and more.

Recent UFO Whistleblower Stories

June 3/23 Former US Intelligence Officer, David Grush Come Forward as Protected US Government UFO Whistleblower has documentation that proves the US Government is in the possession has 12 non-human recovered spacecraft and several alien bodies that piloted the crafts.

Former Marine Michael Herrera tells DailyMail.com that he saw a UFO being loaded with weapons while serving in Indonesia in 2009. Herrera claims an Air Force lieutenant colonel told him, 'You're not allowed to talk about what happened. You will go to prison, or you will die'.

Boswell, Josh. 2023. "Marine Vet Breaks 14-Year Silence to Tell of UFO Sighting." https://www.dailymail.co.uk/news/article-12177943/Marine-vet-breaks-14-year-silence-make-astonishing-claim-six-man-unit-saw-UFO.html.

."1975 Interview with a Man Who Claims He Was Abducted by Aliens." n.d. Www.youtube.com. https://www.youtube.com/watch?v=SjlzeYiGLzc

The U.S. Government's Opportunity for Transparency

This section argues that disclosure of the UFO and ET truth is necessary to end government secrecy and reclaim lost scientific progress. Advanced technologies have been suppressed for power and control, while trillions of taxpayer dollars have funded unacknowledged special access programs. Disclosure may bring initial ridicule but ultimately restore trust through transparency and benefit humanity with new energy and medical technologies. However, those in power wish to maintain control and the status quo. Public demand for open hearings and whistleblower testimony will ultimately force the government's hand toward disclosure.

ABOUT THE AUTHORS

Tucker G.

Tucker in his Bottle House at school

Tucker is currently a 5th grade student who has had extensive exposure to UFO information over several years. He likes researching aircraft and has personally seen UFO anomalies with night vision in Sedona, AZ and his backyard. His favorite subject is science. He is pictured sitting in a plastic bottle house in a plastic bottle chair made by Grand Bob in front of his school May/23 that he helped assemble for his classmates for a special ecology project. He loves riding his bike, swimming, and playing with his friends next door. This is his first book.

Dr. Robert Spalding (Grand Bob)

Crashed UFO in his backyard

Dr Spalding is a practicing podiatrist, reserve deputy, retired paramedic and former two term politician. He has authored 10 books including documentary books titled Death By Pedicure, Drug Subs, How to Homeless In Style: 50 Ways to survive on Plastic Bottles in These Economic Times, The Science of Pedicures as well as several children's books including The Kingdom of Fu Fu, The Fu Fus Go To New York and Sara Claus and The Flying Christmas Pigs. Dr Spalding has also written several fictional books seen at SpaldingPublishing.com that includes the Death By Manicure eBook and the new movie script version of Death By Manicure.

He is CEO of MediNail.com and JustForToenails.com and has been featured on Anderson Cooper as well as podcasts bringing attention to nail salon infections and nail salon lawsuits. He Lives on Signal Mountain, Tennessee and spends a lot of time with his grandson Tucker, sharing inventive projects and activities together.